THE CORE STAR

It seemed to have no color at all, in spite of the incredible flux of energies surrounding it.

"It's more like I can *feel* it than see it," Kelly said wonderingly.

"What's coming from it isn't properly light at all," Sergei said. "A thing of that mass should suck up light like a black hole. It's the center of the whole galaxy."

"What's keeping us alive here?" asked Torwald.

I am the alien replied silently.

"Are you satisfied now?" the captain demanded. "We've taken you to where you wanted to go. Can you get us back to human-occupied space?"

There yet remains a task.

"I thought there'd be a catch," Torwald muttered.

This ship must accelerate directly into the Core Star.

Space
Angel

John Maddox Roberts

A Del Rey Book

BALLANTINE BOOKS • NEW YORK

For Frank

Bonny Scartland again!

Prologue

It had fled for a long time and was weakening. The enemy was nearing, and another battle like the last would finish it. Once pursuer, It had become the pursued. It would have to hide.

Beginning with the nearest, It made a broad-spectrum survey of the neighboring stars, gradually broadening the scan until it encompassed a triangular quadrant of the galaxy, with the Center at its apex.

The survey quickly revealed that the Core Star held no intelligence, a condition to be expected in so small a stellar swarm. The planetary vermin would be the dominant intellects when they began to develop. Meantime, It needed a place to hide.

Though here the stars were few and widely separated, one was found that suited Its purposes: a stable, main-sequence star whose system would probably never give birth to intelligent life.

It gathered material from the star and created a

nest. When the hard crust had formed, It assumed the most efficient form and burrowed in. All functions were curtailed save those necessary to maintain Its form.

It waited.

One

Torwald's timer woke him at 0700. For a few minutes he enjoyed the luxury of staring at the ceiling, then rolled out of bed. It was shipout day. As he shaved, the mirror reflected the Spartan simplicity of his surroundings: bunk, table, chair, a small bathroom, all encompassed by walls painted a pleasing neutral color. The room was identical to millions of others in transients' hotels scattered throughout the ports of the inhabited worlds. A spacer seldom needs anything more luxurious.

His bag was already packed at the foot of the bed, and as Torwald hoisted it to his shoulder, he made the ritual last-minute check for overlooked items, then walked down the hallway to the drop and stepped inside. His stomach jumped as the circular platform swiftly descended ninety-five floors. At ground level, he entered a lobby decorated with murals of alien landscapes, an inevitable motif in hotels catering to spacers.

Outside, the ground level of the multilayer city was

almost devoid of traffic. The big people-movers wouldn't be plying the streets for an hour yet. Torwald took a deep breath. The air smelled clean; Earthport must be on one of its periodic cleanup campaigns, he decided. It still didn't make the city any more attractive to him, but he decided to walk to the spaceport anyway. Soon he would be within the narrow confines of a ship, and he wanted to enjoy a walk while he had the chance. He didn't have much use for cities. The ports were all alike, at least on the more developed worlds, and Earthport was no exception: a great, overcrowded anthill towering into the sky.

Toward the spaceport, brick and concrete buildings gave way to structures of a recently developed plastic foam that, when poured into inflated molds, hardened in seconds. Torwald considered it the ugliest architecture he had ever seen, but it was cheap, and a building could be completed in a few hours. All the construction around the spaceport was new because the area had been bombed flat by the Warlord's forces during the War a few years before.

The rest of Earthport was just waking up, but the spaceport and environs worked round the clock. Torwald was looking for a place that served good meals. He always held back enough pay for one final feast before moving out. On most ships, especially the small ones, ship fare became monotonous very quickly.

He stopped before a sign that proclaimed AUTHENTIC ATHENIAN CUISINE and decided to give it a try. He was partial to Greek food, and Greek restaurants abounded in any port city. The interior smelled of roasting lamb and fresh-baked bread. He sat down and ordered an elaborate meal, dictating his choices to a grille set into the table. A few minutes later a servobot rolled up silently on tiny wheels and delivered plates heaped with thin-sliced lamb on rice pilaf, stuffed grape leaves, and pita bread from its heated interior. Torwald dug in. All was delicious and all authentic, even though the lamb probably had been cloned in a laboratory and the grain for the pita bread was from an orbiting agristation. These days little land remained on Earth for farming or grazing. Torwald finished his breakfast with baklava and coffee, the rich honey-and-nut flavor of the pastry neatly offsetting the strong, bitter black coffee. Before picking up his bag, Torwald jotted "Piraeus" in his notebook, giving it four stars.

At the gate of the spaceport the familiar chemical odor hit him. He inhaled deeply; it was reassuring, the smell of his trade. To the uninitiated it was an ungodly stench: solvent, vehicle fumes, fuel for the boosters and the short-haul chemical burners. After several minutes the loop shuttle—a robot tractor pulling a string of cars lined with benches—glided up to the gate and the few home-bound late-shift workers descended. Torwald climbed aboard. He was the only passenger.

The port area covered four square kilometers of perfectly level surface, much of it occupied by hangars, repair docks, and underground machine shops, which Torwald passed through in the shuttle on his way to the terminal. Far out on the launching fields he could make out the lordly shapes of three towering Transgalactics. They were ships of the big lines that had cornered 97 percent of all intersystem trade and transport. Beyond the Transgalactics stood the humbler, lower silhouettes of the tramps. Those were his ships. In the glamour buckets, all was regimented and impersonal; the only way to gain rank was to bootlick all the way up the ladder. It was a system Torwald couldn't stomach—a flaw of personality that had kept him a ranker or probationary officer all the time he was in the Navy.

The shuttle finally stopped at a gigantic dome, the largest spaceport building in all human space, though those of several of the colonies were catching up fast. Torwald entered the terminal and found himself in an immense circular cavern, acres in area. Around its periphery were ticket booths, waiting rooms, gift shops, snack bars, lading offices, Customs and Immigration, hiring offices, and hundreds of others.

The center of the building was filled with display cases and exhibits illustrating the history of space exploration. Torwald wandered among the cases, waiting for the Ship's Personnel Hiring Office to open. He loved this museum. He'd read about it when he was just a boy living on the fjord at Trondheim, dreaming of the day he would go into space. His initiation into spacefaring had been brutal: drafted at sixteen into the Space Navy when the Triumvirate had attacked the Republic. Many of the displays were devoted to the ships of the Triumvirate and to samples of the weaponry of that vicious but mercifully short-lived empire.

When the hiring light on the big board lit up, Torwald sauntered toward the office. The man behind the desk was typical of those who worked for the port authorities or spacing companies but never got into space themselves: neat uniform, bored face. Torwald unclipped the gold spacer's bracelet from his wrist and handed it to the officer, who fed it into his computer console. The bracelet carried his naval and merchant service records—at least the official parts of both. His eyebrows rose fractionally as he read the printout. "There are two Class Ones of the Satsuma Line out there," he said, "and the Four Planet Line *Starvoyager*. With your qualifications, I could line you up with a berth in any of them."

"Not interested. What about the tramps?"

"Oh, sorry," the young officer said affably. "You have a psych problem?"

"Yeah, I hate stuffed uniforms."

"Well, let's see. There's the *Space Angel*. She's looking for a quartermaster. Captain interviewed all day yesterday and rejected everybody we sent over. Granted, they had all been rejected by the lines, but

6

that's getting awfully picky. None of them had your skills, though. I'd say she's your best bet."

"Sounds good. Captain interviewing yet?"

"In about an hour. I'll page you when I get the word."

"Fine. I'll be in the coffee shop." Torwald shouldered his bag and carried it to a locker. Then he fed in a plastic chip and set the spacebag inside, pressing the ball of his right thumb against the glass plate on the door so it could get a reading of his print. That done, he headed for the lift. Torwald picked the port's general coffee shop on Level Six because it was a good place to pick up gossip about the ships in port and the doings of the lines. He found the shop sparsely populated with people who were mostly spacers like himself, wearing the spacegoing garb of dozens of systems, the uniforms of many lines.

Torwald went to the service block nearest his table and punched the button marked COFFEE, BLACK, SWEETENER. A cup rose immediately through the countertop and he carried it to his table. Seated, he tuned his ears to the talk around him. Life had taught him early to speak little and listen always. Though he could tune in on several conversations at once, he heard little of value. The usual rumors that someone had discovered intelligent aliens; that one had made the rounds every six Earth-months, regular as clockwork, for as long as Torwald could remember. Satsuma was planning a merger with the Nebula Line. That might be useful. Mergers that size were illegal. Torwald filed the information away for future reference.

He suddenly became aware of a presence at his elbow.

"Oh, excuse me, sir."

Torwald looked up and saw a boy, about seventeen, stringy and blond, with a thin, undernourished face. He wore a faded government-issue coverall that was too small for him.

"Go ahead and sit," Torwald said, gesturing at the seat opposite him.

"Thanks," the boy responded, sitting down. "Which ship are you with?" He wore a shy smile and was so puppyish that Torwald was tempted to tickle his belly or swat him with a rolled-up journal.

"I haven't found out yet. I'll probably know by this afternoon." He returned his attention to his coffee. The newcomer was staring at him with awe, and that always made Torwald self-conscious.

"You mean, you can just pick a ship and go out with it?"

"Usually," Torwald mumbled. "There aren't many ship's posts I can't fill, except for bridge officer positions, and engineer. If there are three ships in port, I can usually ship out on one of them." He hoped that that would end the conversation. His hope was futile.

"I've been trying to get one to take me on for a year," said the boy, bitterly.

"What's the problem?"

"No experience. They won't take you without experience. How can I get experience unless I get a job on a ship?"

"Easy," said Torwald. "Join the Navy. That's where I learned spacing. You'll get plenty of ship experience there. When you get out, you'll have your Able Spacer's bracelet." He held up his own.

"I try about once a week," the kid said miserably. "These days, they want you to have a university degree, and I have a slight astigmatism in my left eye. They don't want anybody with a physical defect."

"That's tough, kid. When I went in, they counted your arms and legs. If it all added up to four, you were in. If you could read, that was a plus. That was during the War, of course. They weren't being picky back then."

"That's just it—with the War over, there're too many spacers and not enough berths. The Navy's on peacetime status and only taking university graduates. No way for me to get into space." His face fell.

"What do you do?" Torwald asked to change the subject. "I mean, when you're not haunting the port? What do your parents do?"

"No parents," the boy said with a touch of bravado. "I'm on my own. I was raised in a State orphanage until I was sixteen, then they kicked me out. Too many orphans since the War."

"So what have you been doing?"

The boy shrugged. "Odd jobs. I sweep up around here sometimes. I get a State dole twice a week. They don't let me starve, at least."

"*Spacer First Class Torwald Raffen, report to captain of independent cargo vessel* Space Angel *for interview*," came the disembodied voice of the PA system.

"That's for me," Torwald said, getting up. "Been nice talking to you, kid. Good luck." He walked away without looking back. Torwald wasn't trying to be callous—indeed, he truly felt sorry for the boy. They were just too many of them: kids who wanted to get into space so desperately that it could hurt a spacer just to look at them. There was nothing a man could do. Torwald left feeling disgustingly lucky.

He walked to the ship. He enjoyed crossing space-port docks, and the captain probably wouldn't mind. There would be few qualified men putting in for a job on an elderly tramp freighter. He passed several immense Satsuma Line vessels: lovely ships, even if he couldn't stand to serve in them. The Class Ones had been the workhorses of the line for a number of years. Rumor had it that they were soon to be replaced by something called a Supernova that was to be the most advanced spacecraft ever built, but Satsuma was keeping the project under wraps. Past the Satsumas Torwald came upon the *Starvoyager,* an immigrant ship, ready to ferry thousands from overcrowded, war-torn Earth to some roomier world that offered a chance of a better life.

The tramps, shuttles, and small-line ships were another matter. They were cramped, carrying crews of no more than a couple dozen at most. Scarred and battered, they were usually obsolete castoffs, sold at auction when one of the lines laid in a new fleet of up-to-date ships. To Torwald, they were more beautiful than the finest new craft. They were the ships he had chosen to spend his life in.

Last in the line stood the *Space Angel*. Her position told Torwald something about her recent prosperity. This far from the main buildings, the docking fees were cheaper. She was a real antique, her once glossy sides now dulled after years of collision with drifting space dust. He knew from her name that she had once belonged to the old Angel Line, back in the days when a line had consisted of an owner, a handful of ships, and their semipiratical crews. They had been proud ships in their day: *Star Angel, Angel of Sirius, Guardian Angel, Angel of the Nebulae. Space Angel* was probably the last of that line still spacing. At the top of the gangway, Torwald was greeted by a little man with a big mustache.

"Permission to come aboard," Torwald stated formally.

"Granted," the little man replied. Spacers were creatures of ritual.

Inside, she was so homey that Torwald felt like kicking off his boots. The deck, bulkheads, and overhead were covered with scars from the magnetic plates that spacers had worn on their bootsoles in the days before the invention of the gravity field. He knocked on the captain's hatch and heard a growled "Stand inside."

The captain of the *Space Angel* was a tough-looking woman of about fifty with a thin, intense face and a Sirius V cigar protruding from her teeth. She wore the silly peaked cloth cap affected by many ship's commanders. She held out her hand in the familiar gesture, and Torwald dropped his bracelet into the up-turned palm. She fed it into her console. "Can you handle a shortbeam cutter?" she asked unexpectedly.

"Yes."

"Where'd you learn that?" She seemed surprised. "I rejected a half-dozen applicants yesterday because they couldn't. Were you an asteroid miner?"

"No, I was a POW on Signet. We used 'em in the quarries."

"They trusted prisoners with laser tools?" The captain couldn't mask the incredulous tone of her voice.

"They had explosive collars on us and used remote surveillance. No funny stuff was possible."

"Well, I need a quartermaster. One who can handle a shortbeam and can boss a team using them. Can you do it?"

"Sure."

"All right, Spacer Raffen, you're on. That leaves just one more post to fill."

"What's that?"

"Ship's boy. We still use 'em on these old silos. No mechanization. Our last one grew too old for the job and left the ship on Altair Three. He was a good boy."

"I've got just the kid for you. Boy I just met in the terminal. As bad a case of the spacies as I've ever seen. Could've been me fifteen years ago."

"Bring him aboard."

"He'll need outfitting."

She reached into the console and extracted a plate of thin metal, handed it to Torwald. "That'll see to his outfitting," she said. "Expenses will be charged against his wages. Bring him back in two hours. We lift off at 1200 sharp."

Torwald saluted and walked away with the ship's credit plate in his pocket. Had he been so inclined, he could have charged his own ship with the plate. He knew he'd signed on with a good captain, at least.

Kelly sat in the coffee ship, brooding over his cup,

which was by then half-empty and quite cold. He thought of the spacer who had spoken with him: a tall, lean man, slightly graying, who moved with the easy grace of one who spent his life adjusting to the varying gravities a spaceman encounters. He had worn the gray coverall and battered boots of a man who worked the independent freighters. That was the service Kelly most wanted to get into—taking on cargo where they could find it, delivering it wherever it was to be sent, then waiting for another contract. The tramps had no home and followed no schedule. Kelly would have settled for a job on an Earth-Luna packet, though—anything to get into space!

Kelly felt a tap on his shoulder, and he looked up. It was the spacer again.

"Come on, kid. You've got a berth on the *Space Angel*."

Within a block of the spaceport dozens of surplus stores catered to spacers. The end of the War had dumped millions of tons of surplus gear on the market, and the shops had sprung up overnight. Ideal places for a spacer to outfit himself cheaply. Torwald headed toward the most reputable-looking of these establishments.

"First," Torwald said, "something to stash it all in." The proprietor brought a spacebag in the glossy gray-black favored by the Navy toward the end of the War. Torwald's own bag was the more traditional dark blue.

Torwald rubbed his palms together. "Now, some protective gear." He was enjoying this, and Kelly was delighted with the amassing of the specialized equipment of his new trade. They went to a section where protective clothing was hung from racks or mounted on stands, everything from antipersonnel-missile-resistant vests to suits of articulated plates made from hardened ceramic fiber. Torwald picked out a one-piece coverall of armor cloth.

"Is that for stopping bullets?" Kelly asked.

"Well, partly. But, you'll be going places where thorns and fangs and stickers and stingers and the like are deadlier than any bullet. That's what the armor cloth is for, mainly. Do you have a knife?" Kelly took one out of his pocket: a spring-blade model, cheaply produced. "Get rid of it. That's only useful for sticking people. I'll find you a better one." He checked the display case at the front of the shop, finally choosing a heavy-bladed sheath knife and a small folding pocket model with several tools in the handle besides the knife blade. "These'll do just about anything. Besides which, if necessary, you can always stick people with them."

Then Torwald selected cold-weather gear, a wrist chrono and calculator, work gloves, clothing—all the necessities for a spacer's bag. Last of all, Torwald took Kelly to the rear of the shop, where the footwear was kept. They rummaged around for a few minutes while Torwald gave him a running lecture on the virtues of good boots.

"You might not think so, kid, but boots are more important than any other item of a spacer's equipment. That's because you never know when you may be set afoot, or in what terrain, or in what climate." Kelly didn't like the sound of the expression "set afoot."

"Besides," Torwald continued, "a spacer has very little to do with space, any more than a sailor has with water. It's just something to get across to reach the planets, where the jobs are. And on the ground, you need boots. Aha, jackpot!" With that exclamation, he pulled a pair of boots from a bin. "Genuine pre-War unissued Space Marine boots!"

"How can you tell they're pre-War?" Kelly asked, sorting through the bin to find a pair that fit. Torwald turned a boot sole-up.

"See those little threaded holes? That's where they used to screw in the magnetic plates. They haven't used those plates in fifty years, but the Navy required that the mounts be left there in case of equipment

13

failures. When the War came along, they dropped that reg, and a lot of quality, to cut costs. These boots will last you a lifetime."

At the entrance of the shop, Kelly caught sight of himself in a full-length mirror. He saw himself as he had always dreamed, wearing a spacer's coverall and boots. The coverall hung slack from his thin frame, and the effect was that of a boy dressed up to look like a spacer. He still didn't feel like one. Then Kelly noticed Torwld reflected over his shoulder in the mirror, grinning at his self-absorption.

"Suit's a little big," Kelly said to disguise his embarrassment.

"You'll fill out if this ship's any kind of feeder. I imagine she is. That captain didn't strike me as the kind who'd keep a cook on the ship who didn't know the job."

They returned to the terminal by foot, Kelly working hard to avoid a first-voyager's swagger. Torwald picked up his own spacebag from the locker and they caught a shuttle to the ship. All the way Kelly gaped around him. He had never been allowed onto the field before, and he wasn't really sure that everything was actually happening. When the shuttle drifted up to the *Space Angel*'s dock, Kelly gazed lovingly at her space-scoured sides, her shock absorbers, pitted by contact with the soil of who knew how many thousands of worlds. From the tip of her bluntly tapering nose to the bottom of her landing gear, she was as beautiful to him as the most magnificent palace he had ever dreamed of.

Torwald led the boy up the ramp and went though the permission-to-board ritual again, this time for Kelly. As a member of the crew, Torwald no longer needed permission to board. The gangway ended at a curving ramp that arched upward to meet the opposite wall. Torwald climbed it with practiced ease, but Kelly stumbled and felt his stomach flip as the ship's gravity-field took hold of him. The "wall" they had been advancing toward became the deck, and the ship, which stood upright on its shock absorbers, all at once seemed horizontal. Kelly looked back, only to find that the concrete of the landing field now towered vertically and that the man at the top of the gangway seemed to be standing horizontally, in defiance of gravity. It was a dizzying view, so Kelly looked quickly away and followed Torwald's retreating back.

They emerged from the entry lock into a narrow companionway and turned right. The companionway turned into a catwalk that stretched across a cavernous hold, then transformed into a companionway again, one lined with doors, some bearing labels like CARGO CRANE, HYDROPONICS, LAUNDRY, BATH; other doors bore no labels. When Torwald and Kelly were far forward on the ship, Torwald took a ladder leading to the upper deck. The ladder ended a few paces from the bridge. Torwald knocked at the hatch again.

"Stand inside," They entered.

"So, this is the new boy?" The woman looked Kelly up and down, without expression. "What's your name?"

"Kelly, ah, Ma'am."

"The proper form of address is Captain or Skipper. There's also Gertie, but I'll kick your behind the length of this ship if you ever use it while aboard. On this ship, Skipper is customary. Kelly what? Do you have another name?"

"No, Ma—Skipper. It was the only name I had when the orphanage picked me up in the refugee camp, so . . ."

"Kelly it is, then," she said, punching some keys on her console. With a click, a thin, flexible gold band extruded from a slot. She took the band and clipped it around Kelly's right wrist.

"You are now a spacer aboard the tramp *Space Angel*. Your rank is Probationary Spaceman, Second Class. Once per ship-month you and the rest of the crew will turn in your bracelets to me to have your record updated." She had been businesslike to begin with, but her next instructions were even more so. "You will both now give me your personal sidearms."

Without comment, Torwald reached into his bag and retrieved two holstered pistols. Kelly's eyes widened at the sight of them. One was an ordinary slug gun that fired a high-velocity metal missile—the kind most police carried. The other was the one that made Kelly blink. It was a Service laser, and ex-officers of the Services were the only civilians allowed to carry them on Earth. The skipper took the pistols and turned to Kelly.

"No sidearms?" she asked.

"Just the knives we got at the surplus shop. Do you want those?"

"No, you can keep them as long as you don't use them on your shipmates. Any beam or high-velocity slug weapons, however, must be turned over to the ship's master to be locked in the arms safe before liftoff. If, later, you are found to have such a weapon in your posession, I can cycle you out the airlock without benefit of life-support system." She gave Kelly a few seconds to absorb that great, grim truth, then continued in a lighter tone. "Now, why don't you two go down to the mess and meet your new shipmates?"

They turned to leave the bridge. Over the hatch, Kelly saw the chronometer and read it automatically: 1108, 27 March 2195. A date he'd never forget.

The rest of the crew was gathered around a big rectangular table, drinking coffee and tea. Torwald found a vacant seat and sat down. After hesitating self-consciously, Kelly did the same. Torwald opened the conversation: "Torwald Raffen, quartermaster. This is Kelly, new ship's boy. Call me Tor."

"Ham Sylvester," offered a great black gorilla of a man at one end of the table. The other end, the captain's seat, was unoccupied. "I'm mate and ship's husband." This last was an ancient rank still sometimes used on old ships. Sylvester's smile looked like a piano keyboard. He gestured toward a stunning woman on his left. "This is Michelle LeBlanc, med officer and cook." She smiled radiantly. Kelly could see that Torwald was hooked already.

"Achmed Mohammed, chief engineer and pilot of our atmospheric craft." This was from the little man with the big mustache who had been at the top of the gangway when they boarded. He gestured toward a rather chubby red-headed boy a year or two older than Kelly, who sat next to him. "This is Lafayette Rabinowitz, my assistant."

"Finn Cavanaugh, navigator and distiller," said a tall, black-haired and dark-eyed man who sat next to Lafayette.

"Bertrand Sims," an elderly white-haired man next to Finn announced. "I am supercargo, accountant, and philosopher. The exotic beauty seated across from me is Nancy Wu, officer of Communications and Hydroponics and sometime specialist in alien botany." Petite, raven-haired, and almond-eyed, Nancy seemed far too young to be a ship's officer.

"Does everybody double up on duties here?" asked Torwald.

"Usually," Ham replied. "We're a multitalented bunch. Michelle's a zoologist, Finn's a chemist, I'm a heavy-weapons specialist, Bert knows history, Nancy plays the violin, and Achmed's a holographer. What do you do besides what you signed on for, Torwald?"

"Should I tell you? I'll get roped into a lot of stuff that's outside my duties."

"That's for sure," Ham said blandly. "But you might as well own up to it now. We'll find out eventually."

"Well, just about everything. I was on solo, two and three-man scoutships for most of the War. That took training in just about every ship's position. I'm good at reconnaissance and charting, I know a little geology, and I can handle mining and quarrying. I can pilot atmospheric craft and small watercraft. I can handle light weapons and explosives."

"That's good," said the mate. "With a crew this size, we can use as many capabilities as we can come by. What was your last ship?"

"The *Purple Turkey*. She was a small prospector for Orion Metals and Crystals. The company went bust and the ship was put up for auction."

"Their loss is our gain." Ham turned to Kelly, "Son, you're about to learn spacing from the bottom up. Who wants him first?" He looked around the table.

"Dibs!" said Achmed. "Lafayette and I are going to do a complete overhaul and cleaning of the engine room once we're in space. We can use another hand."

"I'll come down and give you a hand if I can spare the time," said Torwald.

"Appreciate it," said the Arab. The intercom bonged.

"Up ship in five minutes," Ham announced. "Secure those cups. Lafayette, escort Kelly to his quarters and show him how to prepare for lift-off. Torwald, you come with me."

Kelly followed Lafayette from the mess. They descended the ladder to the lower-deck companionway, then scuffled quickly over the catwalk through the hold. Just past the hold, Lafayette opened a hatch that revealed a cramped cubicle outfitted with a folding bunk, a table, and a chair. Kelly stretched himself on the bunk at a gesture from the older boy.

Lafayette drew two broad straps across Kelly's belly and thighs, leaving his arms outside. "These aren't really necessary, Kelly, but the safety regs say you have to be strapped in when you take off. With the grav field on, you don't usually feel much. My cabin's just across the companionway, and Achmed's in the one next to mine. You can unstrap when you hear the next *bong*." With that, he darted out, closing the hatch behind him.

Kelly waited tensely, still unable to believe that it was all happening. Less than two hours before, he had been moping in a spaceport café, no closer to space than on the day he was released from the orphanage. Now, he had a berth aboard a tramp freighter preparing to take off for who knew where. He was terrified that, the dream over, he would awaken on a bunk in a State transient house.

The *Space Angel* began to vibrate, and Kelly felt a slow, directionless pressure that lasted several seconds, then stopped, to be replaced by a feeling of almost-weightlessness. Suddenly, normal gravity resumed. In a perfect artificial-gravity field, acceleration should be undetectable except by instruments, but the new ship's boy was becoming aware that nobody had developed a perfect grav field yet.

At the next *bong,* Kelly unstrapped, rose, and examined his cabin. *His* cabin! He had never had a private room in his life. The closest he had ever come was sleeping under bushes in a park out of sight of other people. The compartment was a small Spartan chamber, but he wouldn't have traded it for a suite in the most luxurious hotel on Earth. This was a spacer's cabin, perhaps four paces long and three wide, the bunk, small desk, and chair folding neatly against the pale-green bulkhead. Former occupants had left their mark: welded to a bulkhead was a hook that must once have held a punching bag; someone had laboriously engraved an alien landscape above the bunk, apparently using manual chasing tools.

He shook his head as he surveyed his new domain, remembering the orphanage, the State transient houses he had lived in; long dormitory halls lined with stacked bunks, never any privacy, and the inevitable thefts and victimization by gangs. He was still musing when Torwald's head appeared through the hatch.

"Got your stuff stowed?"

"I just got out of the bunk a minute ago."

"You'll never cut it in space if you're going to move so slowly, Kelly. Here, your clothes go in this locker." Torwald opened a door into the bulkhead opposite the bunk. He helped Kelly hang his clothes and showed him where to stow his personal belongings. There was pathetically little to put away. They were interrupted by Finn, the navigator, who stuck his head through the hatch.

"Come forward to the laundry and draw your linen, you two. Torwald, the laundry'll be in your charge now, by the way."

"I figured that. The quartermaster usually gets stuck with the odd jobs that don't fall into anyone else's realm of competence."

When Kelly returned with his linen, Torwald showed him how to fold his bunk neatly into its wall slot, then disappeared. Kelly gave his room a final fond glance, then he wandered forward to the mess, where he found Ham and the skipper reviewing some paperwork. The skipper looked up and caught sight of him.

"Kelly, why don't you give Michelle and Tor a hand in the galley?"

"Aye, aye, Skipper," Kelly said, feeling very space-manlike. He found Michelle and Torwald sweating away in the cramped galley. An unfamiliar but delicious odor hung in the air.

"What's that smell, Torwald?" Kelly asked.

"That's fresh bread baking, can you believe it, kid? We landed in a gold mine!"

"Of course I'm baking bread," Michelle said. "As long as the flour holds out, anyway. Kelly, get some plates out and set the table. Tor, fetch three onions from the lower bin, there, and begin chopping them up." Torwald tied on an apron and set to work while Kelly tried to figure out where the plates were secured. When he returned from setting the mess table, he found Torwald bent over a retractable chopping board with his sleeves rolled up.

Michelle was staring at his exposed wrists, which were encircled by bands of thick scar tissue.

"My God! Where did you get those?"

"Never seen manacle scars, Michelle? You should see the ones on my ankles. Leg irons are heavier than manacles."

"I'd heard they did things like that to POWs, but I didn't believe the stories," she said, with a slight shudder.

"You shouldn't believe all the propaganda you hear; nevertheless, some of it's true."

Kelly had seen similar scars on discharged veterans in Earthport, and he had heard some of their stories —enough to realize that Torwald must be an exceptional mental and physical specimen to have survived such treatment with his mind and health intact.

Torwald and Michelle worked together smoothly. Both were proficient from long experience at producing large meals from the tiny space of a ship's galley. Kelly was kept busy hunting up utensils while Torwald prepared the ingredients and Michelle did the cooking.

"I just remembered something," said Michelle. "Kelly how many places did you set?"

"Ten."

"Set another. There's a man aboard you two haven't met yet. He's a factor or something for the company we've contracted with for this voyage."

"Just what is our job this trip?" Torwald asked. "The holds are empty."

"It's all very hush-hush. The skipper and Ham wouldn't say anything before we left Earth. We're supposed to find out after dinner."

Little was said during the meal, but everyone occasionally glanced at the man seated to the skipper's left. He was a serious little man, balding and paunchy, obviously not a spacer.

Though he had never eaten so well in his life, Kelly was relieved when the meal was finished, because he found the exigencies of spacer table manners nerve-wracking. First, Lafayette had rebuked him for

21

passing the salt with his left hand: many spacers came from cultures that forbade handing things with the left hand, so the custom was generally observed throughout the spacing community. When Kelly later passed a plate piled with sliced ham—carefully using his right hand—to Achmed, the boy was surprised to learn that both the engineer and the skipper belonged to faiths that did not permit them to touch pork. Kelly was thoroughly mortified by the time the meal ended and was grateful when the skipper introduced the stranger.

"This is Sergei Popov, factor for Minsk Mineral. He'll be along to supervise the operation we're embarking upon. Suppose you outline the project for the benefit of the crew, Sergei."

"Minsk Mineral is a small, new company," Popov began. "The company was founded by Aleksandr Strelnikov, a geologist. During the War he was a site surveyor for construction outfits building bases in advance of Naval expansion. As geologists will, he made frequent side trips from the construction sites to explore the peculiarities of planetary makeup.

"On Alpha Tau Pi Rho/4, a planet of geological singularity, he made a find. In a range of hills near the base site, he found a stratum of pure diamond crystal so large that it could be cut in slabs. Needless to say, Mr. Strelnikov said nothing about his find to his superiors."

"Shortbeams!" Torwald said.

"I beg your pardon?" Popov looked perplexed.

"When I was interviewed, the skipper asked if I could handle a shortbeam cutter."

"Precisely. Your quarrying skills will be necessary when we reach our destination. Now, where was I? Oh, yes! When Strelnikov returned home at the end of the War, he found some supporters. Together, they scraped up enough financial capital to form Minsk Mineral. For camouflage, we have spent several years working small claims for marginal profit. Now, we go after the big prize. We filed a mineral claim to this small site, supposedly on wildcat speculation. With the proceeds from this voyage, we'll take the mineral option for the entire planet. We decided to hire a tramp for the project in order to escape the notice of our very powerful competition."

He had their full attention. Diamond crystal was one of the most valuable of natural materials, in heavy demand by hundreds of industries. The scent of a pure stratum on an unclaimed world would bring the big mining interests down on it like piranhas. If they could get a full cargo off that world and on the market before they were detected, they would be rich and safe.

"Minsk," the skipper said, "has cut the *Angel* in for a decent share of the profits of this voyage, plus a generous bonus for every member of the crew." At once it was clear that there was no regular ship's hire. If the voyage failed, the ship would be insolvent and they would all be stranded when they reached port. "Any objections?"

"Hell, no," Torwald ventured when nobody spoke up. "When you roll for the big stakes, you take the big risks."

"Why didn't Strelnikov come along personally?" Finn asked.

"Unfortunately, Mr. Strelnikov was blinded during the fighting on Li Po. It will be several years before his new optics are reliable enough for him to space again."

"Any more questions?" the Skipper asked. There were none. "All right, then, Lafayette, you and Kelly wash up after meals. We'll let the artists handle the preparation. Torwald, you'll be Michelle's assistant in the galley from now on." There was no objection from Torwald.

"Tor," Ham said, "tomorrow, familiarize yourself with the supply room. That's your new bailiwick and it's a mess. Among other things, there's a set of shortbeam cutters in there that we picked up at an auction on Earth. They were operative then. You'll have to maintain them as best you can."

"Any other business?" asked the skipper.

"One thing," Michelle chimed in, "Kelly, take this," she tossed him a flat metal box, about five centimeters on a side, with a metal chain. "Wear that around your neck at all times from now on. Those are your tracetabs. They contain all the trace elements your body needs. There are about three thousand tabs in that box. If we go on xenorations, you'll need them."

Kelly seemed puzzled.

"There are about a thousand planets," Sims explained, "that supply native food edible by humans. On maybe half a dozen of them, all the trace elements necessary for human survival are present in the food."

"If the soil and atmosphere are comparable to Earth's," Michelle continued, "native flora and fauna may give you all the protein, carbohydrates, and vitamins you need, but trace elements can be hard to come by. You'll die just as dead from lack of magnesium, phosphorous, or any number of other elements as from lack of water. If you get stranded on a xenoworld, that box can be your lifeline. Always keep it filled."

Kelly looked down at the box in his palm, then he slipped the chain around his neck. It made him feel a bit more like a real spacer. "Thanks," he said. "And my compliments to the chef. I never ate like that in my life."

"Gallantry, yet," said Michelle, smiling. "If that's true, they must not have fed you very well where you came from."

"They starved us," Kelly said seriously.

"Enjoy the good life while you can," Achmed chimed in. "Pretty soon we'll be out of fresh rations and on freezedrys, and when those run out we'll be

24

eating concentrates unless we're lucky enough to find edible native stuff."

"Ah . . ." Kelly started, unsure that he should say anything.

"Speak up," the skipper urged. "We're all ship-mates here."

"This may sound pretty dumb."

"Go ahead." Bert grinned "Everybody gets to say six dumb things on his first voyage. It's an old custom."

"Well, it's just that, here I am in space, and I haven't seen space yet. I mean, not space, but the stars, and, you know—what I guess I'm saying is, is there a window or porthole or something on this ship? So far, it's like being in a building; just not very real. If I could just see the stars, I'd know I was really here."

"Why, to be sure," Finn said, "there's an old navigator's bubble that opens off my instrument compartment. When the *Space Angel* was built, it was still required that there be a place where the navigator could take visual sightings if the instruments failed, though I never heard of such things being any use for charting a course in deep space. When you've finished your galley chores, drop in and I'll open her up. I've not had a look at the stars in a score of voyages."

"I'll be along too, if you don't mind," Bert said. "It would be nice to resurrect the old thrill of being in space. At my age, such nostalgia has a rejuvenating effect."

In all, eight of the ship's company showed up at the observation bubble. A circular area five meters in diameter, its instrument consoles had long since been ripped out, and the air was musty with disuse. Ham brought a box of Taurus cigars, Bert several bottles of wine and some glasses. Nancy arrived with her violin. While the Communications officer tuned up, Torwald whipped out his knife, produced a corkscrew, and began opening bottles.

"Never be without a corkscrew," he instructed Kelly. "It's a tool of survival required throughout the civilized portions of the galaxy."

Kelly sat on the carpeting covering the floor, looking up. Overhead stretched a dome of near-invisible glassite through which the stars and planets shone with a clarity never seen by ground-dwellers. Finn began to point out to Kelly the principal stars and name the planets.

Bert took it upon himself to expound philisophically. "My boy, out there you see the Universe, with a capital *U*. Of course, you have always been able to see the universe by looking in any direction. But, out here, you perceive it with a clarity lacking in any environment encumbered by an atmosphere. And let me tell you, it is strange and enigmatic."

"Weird is a better word," said Ham.

"Things happen out here," Finn nodded in agreement, "which I would consider unbelievable if they happened anywhere on Earth—except, perhaps, in Ireland."

"Oh, no," Michelle whispered to Torwald. "Now they're going to bombard the poor kid with spacers' folklore."

There was a brief pause, them a deep voice asked in sepulchral tones, "Son, have you ever heard of the Blue Lights?"

"I think I read about them somewhere, Ham."

"Well, they're little balls of blue flame that infest a ship just before some disaster occurs. I've known spacers who've seen them."

"And then, there are the Ghost Ships," Finn added while mixing his wine with the contents of a small flask he carried in a hip pocket. "Old ships bearing the names of vessels that never reported home, and they appear to men on doomed expeditions. I saw one once."

"I thought you never came out to the observation bubble, Finn."

"I've a confession to make, Kelly. Secretly, I've often come out to the Navigation bubble to look at the stars and meditate. Once, during the War, I was serving as navigator on a cargo transport supporting the Li Po invasion. On the night before H-Hour, I was reclining in just such a bubble as this one. On a Navy ship, it's just about the only place a man can find some privacy and be safe from his superiors, since most of them don't even know the bubble exists. Suddenly, before my eyes, the specter of a ship appeared: one of those knobby, old-fashioned affairs, all tubes and spheres. Great rents marred her sides, and you could see the bones of the dead inside. Her bridge was lit by a red light, such as they used on the old ships, and enclosed in glassite. Across her nose I could just read the name *Nevsky*. I later learned the *Nevsky* disappeared during a routine run to Titan in 2022, with some of Earth's greatest scientists aboard. The next day—well, everybody knows what happened at Li Po."

Unable to control himself, Bert exclaimeed, "Finn, were I not an old spacer, well versed in the strangeness of the spaces between the stars, I would call you a most thoroughgoing Irish liar. As it is, I shall merely reserve my judgment."

"You don't need to believe Finn or Ham, Kelly," Torwald said, "but before you've been out too long, you'll have seen some strange things." The others nodded their heads in agreement. "The first thing you need to cultivate is a mind open to any possibility, because *anything* is possible out here. You abandoned the word impossible back at the pad when we left."

None disputed this great truth.

Nancy, tuned to her satisfaction at last, broke into a rhapsody by Kallió, the only major composer ever to be a spacer. She followed up the Kallió piece with others by Debussy, Ravel, Respighi, and Holst. Of Earth's composers, these were the spacers' favorites;

their impressionistic melodies evoked the flavor of life between the stars better than any others, even though the composers had lived out their lives bound to Earth.

Onc by one the crew began to retire to their cabins. The violin was put away, the empty bottles picked up, the aroma of cigar smoke faded as the smoke trailed down the ladder to the Navigation compartment. Fially, no one was left in the bubble except Kelly, looking at the stars.

Two

Kelly passed through the hatch marked ENGINE ROOM. Faded letters below said UNAUTHORIZED PERSONNEL KEEP OUT. Kelly wondered if the restriction applied to him, decided it didn't, and entered.

The room was brightly illuminated, and its bulkheads were painted stark white, in contrast to the rest of the ship, which had been painted in various colors and patterns according to the whims of former skippers. Toward the rear, two pits contained the lower halves of the main thrusters. Between them was slung the tapering cone of the Whoopee Drive. Achmed and Lafayette had stripped the cowling from the off-duty thruster and were scrubbing it down with a variety of implements.

"Hop in and get to work!" Achmed shouted. "Take Lafayette's side." Kelly dropped into the well next to the red-headed boy and reached toward a sonic disruptor of the kind he had seen used on Earth to clean buildings. Lafayette slapped his hand away before he could touch the instrument.

"Naughty, naughty. Kiddies don't play with power tools in the engine room. Here, take some of this and start scrubbing." He thrust a wad of steel wool into Kelly's hand. "That's more your speed. Now, get to work."

Kelly scrubbed at the piled-up engine gunge, fuming silently. It was like that all morning. The older boy kept finding fault with Kelly's work and passing Kelly the dirtiest jobs. Kelly refused to let the hectoring destroy the enjoyment of his first real spacer's work. He had performed harder, dirtier labor before, so the necessarily grimy work of engine maintenance didn't bother him. Eventually Achmed called Lafayette over to his side of the thruster and Kelly heard a brief, muffled exchange before Lafayette returned. For the rest of the job, Lafayette dropped the bullying, but Kelly resented Achmed's interference. He thought he could take care of himself.

Toward the end of the morning shift, Torwald dropped in. "I've just been to the supply room, and it's the most disgusting mess I've ever seen. I'm not going to try to tackle it until Kelly's free to give me a hand." He picked up a disruptor and dropped into the pit next to Kelly. Lafayette had crossed to Achmed's side, to dismantle a coolant valve. "Who was my predecessor, anyway—a Vegan swamp farmer?"

"A man named Krilencu," Achmed replied. "He had an excessive fondness for the bottle in his later years."

"It shows." Torwald grimaced. "Why did the skipper keep him on if his veins were full of thruster fuel?"

"He spaced with her wing during the War. They say he was a good man back then. Her wing saw some heavy combat. A lot of people took to the juice when things got so rough it looked like nobody was going to live through it. Some of them couldn't stop when it was all over. I guess the skipper felt kind of responsible."

"Well, her loyalty's commendable," Torwald commented. "But, he's left me with the lousiest job of sorting and accounting I've ever contemplated."

"A man with all your talents should find it easy," Achmed said blandly.

"Hah! See if I ever come down to help you clean our lousy engines again." He turned to Kelly. "Well, kid, how do you like your first taste of real spacing?"

"I love it!" Kelly's teeth flashed white in his grimy face. "But, wouldn't it have been easier to do this job in port?"

"Easier, sure," Torwald noted, "but not as efficient. A ship on the ground is earning nobody any money, not the owners nor the crew. Any job that can be done on shipboard by crew labor and with ship's equipment should be done en route to pickup or delivery. That's the most efficient use of a ship's time."

"Coffee break!" Achmed yelled, and all four of them lined up at the engine room coffee urn. After several minutes of friendly banter about Torwald's quartermastering problems, Torwald kidded Achmed about the sweatshop the engineer was running.

"It'll be cooler when we cut in the Whoopee Drive," Achmed said to Kelly, gesturing toward the drive housing. Intrigued by the strange object, Kelly walked over for a closer look at the drive mechanism, a big spindle suspended in line with the ship's long axis. It was featureless except for the clear glassite tip within which the boy could make out a revolving crystal Möbius band.

"How does this thing work, Achmed? I heard it won't work within a solar system."

"Damned if I know." The engineer shrugged. "I know how to run it, but I don't know how it runs. Do you know, Tor?"

"Kelly," said Torwald, "there are maybe fifty physicists who can claim to understand the Whoopee Drive, but they understand only the principle which is quite a job in itself. It's like Einstein and relativity; you can learn its effects and harness the principle, but the whys of it are beyond the grasp of human brain power."

"Hah!" Kelly chuckled. "I thought you old spacers were supposed to know everything about ships."

"About *running* them, sure," said Torwald. "But as to what makes them go, that's a job for scientists. We're just glorified proletarians. We may be experts, but space drive isn't our realm of expertise. Look, I'll give you an example: There was never a more skilled professional in the world than the eighteenth- and nineteenth-century sailor. His craft was in making a fragile construction of wood and cloth take him just about anywhere there was water, and a bad sailor meant a sunk ship. They had a knowledge of wind and water a hundred times more intimate than any spacer has of space. Yet few men alive in those days knew why the wind blows, or why the ocean has currents."

Achmed suddenly interrupted. "Speaking of wind, you're pretty long-winded yourself. I never would've expected it."

"Look, I try to pass on to this kid the valuable lessons of a lifetime spent in space, and what do I get? Ridicule! Where's your sense of obligation, Achmed? It's the duty of us old hands to give the young a proper education."

"Between your educating and Finn's tale-spinning, this kid will jump ship at the first port and never set foot on another. Back to work!"

They scrubbed for another couple of hours. Once, they heard a bong from a timer on the bulkhead. Achmed jumped from his well, stripped and stepped under a sonic cleaner. When he was spotless, he opened a battered wall locker, withdrew and slipped on a white robe, then placed a small skullcap on the back of his head. Next, he removed a small rolled-up rug and spread it on the deck. He knelt and began his prayers, facing the thruster exit cones.

When his devotions were over, the Arab changed back into his work clothes and picked up his scrub brush. An hour later, another bong sounded and Michelle's voice called from the intercom: "Torwald, Kelly, report to the galley."

The two cleaned up and found Michelle in the galley, rolling out dough for pies. "The menu features roast beef and Yorkshire pudding today," she announced. "Kelly, get two kilos of dried apples out of the storeroom. Tor, start measuring out the sugar. The recipe's over there." She nodded toward a piece of paper clamped to the bulkhead over the range. Once they had established a work rhythm, Michelle began questioning Torwald and Kelly about their histories, standard procedure for a med officer: survivors of Arcturan Blight could not take penicillin, and quinine-4 would cause a harmless virus from Vega Prime to mutate into a deadly mankiller. The med officer needed detailed medical histories of all crew members, or disaster could result. Kelly presented no problems; he had been under State health care all his life and had never been exposed to alien diseases or conditions. On the other hand, Torwald's history was complex and colorful, and Michelle recorded occasional notes as he spoke.

Once their physiological histories were taken care of, Michelle began to question them about their psychological histories. Kelly found himself unsure whether these were professional questions or the result of curiosity. He did notice that Michelle seemed far more interested in Torwald's background than in his own. Eventually she sent Kelly out to set the table, but he could still hear them talking.

"Ever been married, Tor?"

"Once. My wife was a scoutship officer like me. She was sent out to recon Toth before the landing. Only one ship of her wing returned, and it wasn't hers.

33

We were expendable people in the scoutships. What about you?"

"Twice. The first was a med officer in a hospital attached to the University of Lima. He was killed in a bombing before the Shield was developed. The other was an engineer on a troop transport. We met when I treated him for burns while I was serving aboard the *Asklepios*. He was killed a year later at Li Po." Neither wasted words on empty consolations. Everybody had lost someone in the War. If you tried to console everyone you met, little time would remain for anything else.

After lunch, Torwald told Kelly to find a notebook before joining him in the supply room—there would be a good deal of paperwork for the boy to handle. Kelly headed back to his cabin. Notebooks and scribers had been among the supplies Torwald had dictated back on Earth. Returning with a pad, Kelly was crossing the hold when he noticed a motion from the corner of his eye. Holding tightly to the railing, he leaned over to peer into the dim, cavernous hold below.

There it was again. Something darted across the bottom of the hold. Darted wasn't quite the word to describe the motion—it was more like a waddle, although very quick. And whatever made it was green. Intrigued, Kelly climbed over the railing and slid down a support strut to the bottom. He peered forward through the cylindrical chamber. Something was moving away from him on four feet. It seemed to be about the size of a small dog. Kelly approached the critter cautiously; for all he knew, the thing might be dangerous. Sensing his presence behind it, the creature turned and stood on its hind legs, forelegs dangling barely reaching its round belly. Its flat face had a tiny mouth and an oversized, onion-shaped nose. The head was framed by two furry ears, giving the thing the look of someone wearing a poke bonnet. It had round button eyes, widely spaced. A more harmless-looking creature Kelly had never seen.

"Hey, are you scaring Teddy?" Kelly looked up. The comm officer, Nancy Wu, was staring down over the edge of the catwalk.

"Teddy?"

"Of course, who did you think it was? Bring him up here. He's not supposed to be loose in the hold." Kelly walked up to the creature. Before he could stoop to pick him up, Teddy simply climbed Kelly's trouser leg to the front of his coverall, then installed himself on his shoulder, where he stared down into his face and blinked solemnly. Kelly turned and climbed the ladder. When he was level with the catwalk, Teddy stepped from his shoulder and scampered to Nancy, who scooped him into her arms.

"What were you doing, chasing him? You've scared him half to death." Kelly regarded the creature, which looked about as panicked as the average oyster.

"I wasn't chasing him. I just saw him down there and I was curious. What is he anyway?"

"A Narcissan Teddybear, of course."

"Of course," said Kelly, nodding solemnly, still unenlightened. He wanted to ask more about the creature, but Nancy turned and stalked away. Kelly continued on his way to the supply room and arrived without encountering any more extraterrestrials—or even any terrestrials, for that matter.

"What took you so long?" Torwald asked as the boy entered.

"How come everybody says that?" said Kelly, growing irritated.

"Because you're expected to step lively in space, and you haven't stepped lively enough. On the old seagoing ships, slow crewmen were helped along with a rope's end applied where it would do the most good. You're not back on the block, you know." Torwald turned to rummage through a pile of invoices, and Kelly looked around at the chaotic jumble of the supply room. His eye was caught by a rack of machines standing against a bulkhead. They were shiny-black devices of metal and plastic that looked something like forcebeam rifles, but heavier and larger, each with a complex folding tripod. Kelly reached out to pick one up.

"Don't touch it!" snapped Torwald.

"Huh?" Kelly was startled at the real anger in Torwald's voice.

"Never touch a lightbeam device aboard ship! Remember when the skipper demanded our sidearms, and I gave her my Service laser? That wasn't just for form. You can cut a ship this size clean in two with one of those things—it's expressly forbidden for any crew member to handle a device that can destroy the integrity of the ship's hull. Only the engineer and med officer are exempted, and then only under specific conditions. The skipper even has to be present when Michelle uses her laser scalpel or tooth drill. For that matter, I can't even test these cutters until we make planetfall. That's why we generally make elaborate tests at the point of purchase. Once you've upped ship, it's too late."

"They're shortbeams, aren't they? Why not set it for a half-meter beam and test it? That'd be safe."

"What if it's the depth control that's malfunctioning, dummy?"

"Oh, yeah," Kelly said sheepishly nodding as the light dawned.

Torwald sat down behind a well-worn console and punched a button marked BRIDGE.

"Bridge here. This is Ham."

"Ham, Torwald here. Could you flash me the inventory-control info?"

"Sure, but I don't envy you this job."

Torwald and Kelly soon understood precisely what he meant. As the rows of words and figures progressed across the screen, Torwald's expression turned to one of alarm. He punched for the bridge again.

"Ham, even the computer can't make anything out of these figures, and the last entry is dated March

2187! I heard that my predecessor was a drunk, but I didn't know he was a saboteur."

"Old Krilencu was kind of peculiar," Ham admitted impassively. "He always seemed to know how much of everything there was, and where it was. He just sort of carried everything around in his head."

"Including an ever increasing load of rocket cleaner."

"Nobody said you were going to have an easy job. If you wanted one, you should've shipped on a line vessel." With that, the mate clicked the communicator off.

Torwald glared at the speaker for a moment, then turned to Kelly. "We might as well get started. First, we sort. Clear out a section against that bulkhead opposite the hatch, and we'll put all the planetside equipment there."

During her peregrinations about the galaxy, the *Space Angel* had picked up an incredible assortment of gear, most of which Kelly didn't recognize. There were collapsible tents, heaters, ice axes, machetes, sonic insect-repellers, backpacks, saws, surveying instruments, tools of every sort, and underwater breathing apparatus, cold-weather survival gear, respirators, poisonous-gas filters—things to keep humans alive and working in a hundred environments. There was much more. It all presented an appalling spectacle.

"We've got to catalog all this?"

"No, Kelly *you're* going to sort. I'll catalog. If you're going to learn spacing, this is the place to learn it. Everything that goes into running the ship passes through this department sooner or later. The quartermaster's responsible for all matériel exclusive of cargo. If Nancy needs some wiring for her communications gear, she'll find it here. If the bridge needs new chart thimble blanks, I'll have to order them. Michelle runs the galley, but I'll be buying the rations when we're in port. The quartermaster keeps records of all issues and returns of gear, all expenditures of fuels and perishables—the works. That, of course, apparently didn't apply to my distinguished predecessor."

"I didn't think the job was so complicated." Kelly was clearly intimidated.

"They're all complicated. With luck, we may have this department under control by the time we reach the edge of the solar system and can kick in the Whoopee Drive."

"When will that be?" asked Kelly.

"About two months, this trip."

"That long? Does it take so long to get out of every system?"

"Depends on the star and where you're starting from, Kelly. Two months is about average."

Kelly was a little disheartened. He had pictured a spacer's life involving landings on dozens of planets every year. He hadn't realized there would be so much waiting. "It seems like a long time between planets."

"Don't worry. You won't get bored. We'll keep you occupied."

Torwald proved as good as his word. Kelly spent the better part of the next two ship-months getting the supply room in order, and more was involved than just sorting and shelving. The youth found that Torwald wanted every piece of equipment in perfect working order. There were cleaning and repairing to do. Worn parts had to be replaced, and where no replacements were available, Torwald would fabricate them in the machine shop adjoining the supply room. When the two had finished sorting and refurbishing, every piece of string was accounted for, every axe and machete polished and sharpened. A fair start had been made on the records, but that task at times seemed hopeless. Items listed on the old inventories had disappeared without record, and others seemed to have appeared, equally without documentation. Kelly had to keep duplicate notes on everything, because Torwald said that he didn't trust any ship's computer that could allow such outrages.

On the occasions when he could be spared from his supply room duties, Kelly pulled all the scut details for the other departments. He was rapidly putting the "adventure" of spacing in its proper place—it was difficult to find or nonexistent. The crew treated him with varying degrees of interest. Nancy had not spoken ten words to him since their encounter in the hold. But then, she rarely said anything to anybody. Finn, on the other hand, would regale him for hours with stories of his travels and experiences, most of which Kelly decided were outrageous lies. Lafayette continued to ride him unmercifully whenever Kelly's duties threw them together. On one occasion, he complained of this to Torwald.

"Look, Kelly, traditionally, the newest, youngest man on ship catches hell from the man who was formerly in that position. That's been going on in ships since before Lord Nelson was a middy."

"Lord who was a what?"

"Look it up. Now, get back to work."

The day arrived when they reached the outer rim of the solar system and could go into interstellar drive. Kelly, like all the rest, was a bit light-headed from fasting and using purgatives. The others had assured him that this regimen would make the experience less unpleasant. When the warning came over the intercom, Kelly retired to his compartment, strapped himself on the toilet, and tied a bag over his mouth. One of the physical effects of the Whoopee Drive was that all bodily systems began to behave erratically, causing bowels and bladder to let go and the stomach to convulse in projectile vomiting. Perspiration drenched the body, eyes watered, and the nose streamed mucus. After that came the hallucinations.

The subsonic twang went through the ship, and

Kelly braced himself. It did no good. After the worst
of the convulsions were over, he saw to his horror
that his room swarmed with tiny, metallic termites,
and they were nibbling away at the walls of the cabin.
When they had eaten through the side, he knew he
would die of explosive decompression. They were almost through when the second twang was felt. It was
the cockcrow that made spacers' demons return to
wherever they came from.

When he'd washed up, Kelly slowly made his way
to the mess, where he found the other crew members, like him, a bit pale and shaky. Michelle was
trying to get everyone to eat soup to replace some
of the fluids they had lost.

"Is it always that bad?" Kelly asked Ham in a
hoarse croak.

"Sometimes it's worse. You made it here under
your own power, so it wasn't as bad as it could have
been. Next time, you'll know something of what to
expect, so the transition won't be such a shock."

"You should see what it's like on a thirty-thousand-
man troop transport," said Michelle. "Sometimes we
had to take them through in free fall with nothing but
netting to separate the men."

While Kelly was deciding that perhaps his experience hadn't been so bad after all, the skipper bustled
in, looking no worse than usual. Rumors had it that
some spacers actually *liked* Whoopee Drive transition,
and he suspected that she was one of them.

"Finn," she said," you brought us out right on the
money. We'll be in parking orbit around Alpha Tau
in two hours. Good navigation. My compliments to
your computer." The skipper turned to Popov. "The
landing pad built for the Navy during the War was
abandoned, but they left a beacon. Do you know if
Strelnikov found a suitable landing site near the
crystal?"

"He thought that it might be feasible, but he's no

pilot. He didn't dare ask any of the Navy pilots for fear of arousing suspicion."

"We'll land on the Navy pad, then," said the skipper. "We'll send the atmosphere craft to scout the site. I hope we can locate a good berth there; it would be hell transporting the crystal all the way back to the base.

"All right, then; everybody lay in a substantial meal, we've got work ahead of us. Tor, break out some respirators. Oxygen's a bit thin down there. Michelle, any medical precautions we should take?"

"The Admiralty manual says there's nothing down there a human can catch unless it was left there by the Navy. The primary's a low-radiation type, so the mutation rate is low. No plant life more highly evolved than a giant fern and the highest animal forms are multilegged insect equivalents—none venomous to humans. Gravity's about 10 percent lower than Earth. Just don't go for more than a couple of minutes without a respirator and there should be no problems."

The crew ate with cautious gusto as their stomachs were still suffering residual twinges from transition. After lunch, Kelly went to the navigator's bubble to have a look at Alpha Tau Pi Rho/4. Even from space it was a drab planet, somewhat smaller than Earth, but much older—her seas had shrunk to lakes, clouds few and thin, vegetation just anemic patches of dingy green against the general grayness. Torwald joined him in the bubble.

"The kind of place where Navy men dread being stationed. Oh, well, we didn't come here for recreation, after all. If this deal pays off as we expect, we can spend all the time we care to on a resort world. Kelly, you'll come with me to scout out the crystal formation in the atmosphere craft, so as soon as we land, meet me at the dock. While we're on the ground, the grav field won't be operating abaft the forward hold bulkhead. That makes loading the holds and launching the AC easier, but watch your step when you cross the line. It's a long drop through the hold if you don't catch the ladder." The landing horn honked. "There is it," said Torwald. "Go strap yourself in."

The planet was no more attractive close up than it had been from a distance. Kelly's first good look at an alien world was from the atmosphere craft dock while Torwald and Achmed readied the craft itself.

"Somehow, I expected something more exotic." His voice sounded tinny over the respirator that covered his nose and mouth.

"As habitable planets go," said Torwald, "this one's pretty near the bottom of the barrel."

The surface resembled the dreariest of Earth's desert—rock, sand, and thin, undernourished vegetation. The mountain ranges were worn to nubbins, not an elevation higher than a thousand meters on the whole planet. From the amount of coal the Admiralty survey had found, vegetation had once been abundant on Alpha Tau, but the planet's water vapor and oxygen had slowly leaked into space until only the hardiest life forms could survive. As usual in such cases, the survivors were the most primitive organisms, the ones that had been the least demanding of their environment in the first place. Alpha Tau was a world far gone in senility.

"Not much to look at, is it, Raffen?" Kelly turned to find Popov standing behind him. The Russian was dressed in a geologist's field gear, a tightly rolled chart under his arm.

"No argument there. I can see right now that you're going to have to offer big bonuses to tempt miners to come to this place. I worked better spots as a POW."

"Pile in!" Ham called. Torwald, Kelly, and Popov climbed aboard the AC. The mate spoke briefly with Popov while Torwald and Kelly removed the AC's all-weather top and locked a low, rounded windshield into place around the pilot's area, then he turned to Torwald.

"Torwald, you're our most experienced pilot, so you take the controls."

Kelly sat directly behind the pilot, from where he could study the operation of the AC. When all were belted in, Torwald eased the craft from the bay and took it up slowly for a hundred meters, to get a good look at the landing field. All the prefabs had been removed, except for the small shed housing the beacon. Only rectangular foundations remained to indicate the buildings had ever existed. The outpost was a forlorn sight.

"Where away?" asked Torwald.

"Taking the beacon for a homing point," said Popov, "set course 85 degrees, magnetic, for ninety-seven kilometers." Torwald punched the bearing into the craft's computer, then accelerated. He could have relinquished manual control but preferred to use the opportunity to get the feel of the AC. The dismal landscape sped by below them as they climbed from the shallow basin where the old base had been and headed into the hills.

Eventually Popov gave the word to stop and hover, though the terrain below looked just like all the rest they had passed over. He directed them up a small canyon at low speed, occasionally consulting his chart. Soon, Torwald spotted what they were looking for and pointed toward it.

A jagged slab of glittering crystal protruded from the wall at the end of the canyon like a cantilevered balcony. Below it lay silver fragments that had somehow broken from the main mass. There were few of these, since there isn't much in nature that can break diamond crystal. Torwald brought the AC down as near to the formation as he could maneuver.

They clambered from the AC and trudged up the hillside to the crystal, where they found themselves gazing at the biggest fortune any of them had laid eyes on.

"Utterly unique." Popov seemed somewhat awed.

"How's it unique?" Kelly asked. "I've heard of diamond slab being mined on other worlds."

"Because it shouldn't be here—not on a world this small. Ordinarily, the pressures required to produce such a prodigy are generated only on worlds much more massive. As a geologist, I would have said that such a thing was impossible, but, as our friends have already told you, such words should not be used by spacers. Still, this phenomenon makes as much sense as bananas growing from a saguaro cactus."

"What do you think broke off those pieces?" Ham asked.

"Maybe quakes, maybe a meteorite." Popov shrugged. "It's probably lain exposed like this for a billion years, so it would come as no surprise if it had been hit once or twice. Erosion has been very slow here in recent eras."

"Well," said Ham, "we can speculate to our hearts' content on the way back to Earth. Right now, I'm calling the skipper and telling her to bring the ship in. There's space to land her here, and the canyon floor's sufficiently solid according to the AC seismometer."

After the *Space Angel* arrived, Torwald and Kelly off-loaded the cutters and their mounts, and soon all the equipment had been carted up the hillside by powerbarrow. Bert had supplied templates to guide the cuts, thin plastic patterns that the quarriers would use to shape their slabs precisely. The *Angel's* hold was nearly cylindrical, and Bert did not want to waste a single cubic centimeter of space. When the gear was set up, the skipper ventured out to examine everything. After she was satisfied about the condition of the shortbeam cutters, she turned to Torwald. "How you going to organize your teams?"

"First off, we cut away the impure stuff on the outside of the outcropping. Ham, Finn, and I have the muscle for that. We'll manhandle the cutters and the others can dispose of it. When the pure stuff is exposed, I'll put the cutters on mounts for the fine work. Sergei will have to indicate where the cuts are to be made, and Achmed, Kelly, and Lafayette will cart the slabs back to the ship. Bert will direct storage in the hold, and Nancy can spell us on cutters after they're mounted, if she likes." He did not suggest that Michelle be assigned a ground job. The med officer was never risked if it was avoidable.

"Go to it, then."

Torwald picked up one of the cutters and, for a moment, held it while indulging in a private reverie. Only Michelle, standing by the AC, had an inkling of what was going through his mind. She had seen his psych profile, knew something of his history. She guessed that the feel of the tool was taking him back to Signet and the smell of blood and sweat and dead men in the quarries, the starvation and exhaustion and the never-ending fear.

After a minute, Torwald shook off the mood and made a test cut. A sheet of impure crystal streaked with rocky matrix fell away cleanly. One by one, he tested the other cutters. All worked perfectly. Under Popov's supervision, they were soon cutting away at the outcropping while Achmed, Kelly and Lafayette were disposing of the dross. The debris was worth a fortune as gem and industrial diamond, but it would have to be recovered by the next team when Minsk Mineral established a permanent installation.

Once the worst was cleared away, Torwald set the cutters on mounts while Popov scribed lines on the now flat-surfaced outcropping, using Bert's templates. The slabs were to be cut ten centimeters thick and fifty on a side, rectangular, except for those that were to fit the circular walls of the hold. Each slab weighed nearly twenty kilos, and wrestling them onto the powerbarrows for the ride to the hold was rough work. Ham and Achmed tried to rig up a suction crane to make the loading easier, but the unstable surface of the hillside made it impracticable. Muscle labor was the only answer.

After ten hours of continuous work, everyone was bone-tired, but still stimulated by the prospect of the wealth this voyage would bring.

"Quitting time," Torwald announced suddenly. "Everybody back to the ship—everybody, that is, except you two." He pointed at Kelly and Lafayette. "You get to clean up the site and make sure everything is ready for us to start work in the morning." Both groaned.

When the others had left, Kelly and Lafayette got up from where they had been leaning against a rock and brushed the seats of their coveralls. They began sweeping up and loading the dross into the power-barrow to be hauled away and dumped.

"Hurry it up, kid," said Lafayette. "I'm getting hungry."

Kelly stopped what he was doing. "We're not on the ship now."

"So?"

"I have to take that kind of treatment from you on the ship, but down here I'm not taking it. Back in the State homes, I had to put up with a lot from the dorm chiefs because they had authority backing them up. But they didn't try to pull any of that stuff on me out on the street. They knew better. You'd better learn better, too."

"Oh? What do you propose to do about it?" He placed his palm on Kelly's chest and began to shove, but he had barely touched Kelly when he caught a roundhouse punch to his jaw. The redhead went down and skidded away downslope.

"You've been riding me long enough, Lafayette."

"I'm disappointed in you, kid." Lafayette wiped his mouth, then glanced briefly at the smear of blood left on the back of his hand. "I thought you were coming along pretty well. Now it looks like you've got to be put in your place again." He got up, dusted himself off, and charged. Kelly sidestepped and tripped him, then jumped on his back and tried for a stranglehold. He missed his grip, felt Lafayette's hands get him behind the neck, and found himself tumbling through the air until he landed on his back with the redhead on top. Kelly saw stars as he caught what he presumed to be two swift punches to the face, then he got a hand under Lafayette's chin, forcing his head back and thrusting the stiff fingers of the other hand into his throat.

Lafayette fell away, gagging, and Kelly took the opportunity to push him over on his back and drop a handful of sand into his open mouth. He found, however, that Lafayette wasn't as helpless as he seemed. The older boy threw a double kick into his stomach with both space boots. Kelly flew back, coming up short against the crystal outcrop, his head banging into the unyielding surface. He slid downward until he was in a sitting position. When he caught his breath, he saw that Lafayette was sitting up, spitting the last of the sand-and-blood mixture from his mouth. Kelly derived a qualified satisfaction from the sight. Qualified, because he wasn't feeling much better.

"Had enough, Kelly?"

"What do you mean? You look worse than me."

"I guess I do," Lafayette admitted with a rueful smile. The smile hurt, so he stopped. "Shall we call a truce for a while, kid?"

"No truce. You stop riding me, on *or* off the ship, or we do this every time we're off-ship together. If you can't live with those conditions, we can have at it again, right now."

"All right," Lafayette said after a pause, "it's a deal. Now, let's finish up here."

On board, the others raised some eyebrows as the unkempt duo entered the mess. "What happened to you two?" the skipper asked.

"We fell down the stairs," Lafayette replied. There was no further comment.

After three weeks of labor, the hold was nearly full. The crew were all bent over from the strenuous labor, and those who were not dark to begin with had been heavily tanned by the ultraviolet light of Alpha Tau's sun, which easily penetrated the thin, cloudless atmosphere. The last few days, the quarriers actually worked within the hillside since almost all of the outcrop had been removed. On the final shift, Kelly and Torwald were slicing the crystal face when Achmed arrived with the powerbarrow.

"Bert says there's room for fifteen more slabs," the Arab announced.

"Great!" Torwald said. "We'll finish up and lift for home this afternoon."

"Hey, what's this?" Kelly asked, sounding mystified. He was lifting the slab Torwald had just cut free. Beneath it, glinting in the light of the lamps they had rigged, was the upper surface of something spherical and metallic.

Calmly, after a moment's hesitation Torwald turned to Kelly. "Run to the ship and bring everybody back on the double. There's something weird here."

After a couple of hours, every test the crew could devise to determine the object's significance had been conducted. Nothing they tried yielded any useful data.

"Well, Skipper, it looks metallic, but it doesn't behave like metal. No reagent will touch it, and, besides, the laser didn't cut it."

"Now what kind of substance lets a laser beam go right through it and cut crystal beyond?" the skipper mused while looking at the slab that had topped the thing. It showed a depression that Finn's measurements had shown to be a perfect section of a sphere.

"The beam didn't necessarily go through it," Nancy pointed out. "It may have bent around."

"Well, if it did it once, it can do it again," said the skipper. "Tor, cut away the remaining crystal and let's have a look at that thing. But don't waste more diamond than necessary."

Finn read off some measurements and Torwald set the controls on his cutter. He made three vertical cuts to a depth that should have been at the thing's maximum girth, if it were indeed a true sphere. He then made a horizontal cut at the same depth to meet the others. Gingerly, Ham lifted away the slab. The thing now looked like a globe of liquid mercury, about the size of a soccer ball.

After examining two small instruments that Finn held, the skipper turned to Torwald. "It carries no charge, and it emits no radiation, Tor. See if you can lift it out."

"How about somebody more expendable, Skipper? Kelly for instance. After all, I'm the only quartermaster you've—"?

"Pick it up!"

He picked it up. It lifted easily from its bowl, and Torwald figured its weight at about five kilos. It was silver, but colors chased each other across its surface. It was undeniably beautiful, but the emotions it aroused in the watchers had little to do with aesthetic appreciation. The skipper took the sphere from Torwald and regarded it balefully.

"I'm taking it back to the ship. Finish filling the hold and we'll study this some more when we're on our way."

She left, and the crew increased its work pace, trying to get the rest of the crystal cut and stored. Suddenly, they were all anxious to depart. The operation had been proceeding without a hitch, and suddenly they were thrown a curve. A spacer learns early to distrust intrusive anomalies.

Once again, the crew was gathered around the mess table, but this time they had a new centerpiece. The whatsit sat there enigmatically, in defiance of all common sense. The skipper was fishing for theories to explain the thing.

"Sergei, how old do you figure that crystal stratum is?"

"Well, the planet's primary star is a stable yellow Type G, much older than Sol, and the diamond would have formed at a fairly early period in the planet's life, so, at a minimum, maybe one billion years. More likely two or three."

"And yet," said Bert, voicing what was in all their minds, "this thing looks more like an artifact than a natural phenomenon. Is that a valid possibility, Nancy?"

"Not as far as I know. If Sergei is right about the age, then it predates any alien artifact ever found by a tremendous span." Kelly noted that the usually taciturn Communications officer was talking more today than she had since he had joined the ship. He decided that the sphere must be making her nervous.

"But, how could something like this end up imbedded in a mass of diamond?" the skipper asked. "According to Sergei, even the diamond shouldn't have been there. What do you think, Ham?"

"Well, Gertie, we've seen some strange things in our years in space, but this is one of the best. An enigma literally inside an enigma. I feel we'll get nothing more out of it until we reach Earth. We have no research facilities other than what we've already tried. We'll just have to leave it to the scientists at the XT Phenomena lab."

That evening, there was a great deal of casual visiting and discussing throughout the ship. Everyone was edgy about the strange thing they had found. Kelly was in Bert's cabin, allegedly receiving instruction in space law, but doing nothing of the sort. He liked to visit the old spacer's cabin because it was a museum devoted to Bert's long life in space. He had models of every ship he had served on and souvenirs of every planet he had landed on. Bert felt that his collection was far more interesting than keeping a diary.

Kelly was relaxing on the deck, lying back with Teddy sitting on his stomach. Teddy's stubby-fingered hands were dismantling a ship model, carefully lining the pieces up on Kelly's chest. Bert never scolded Teddy for taking such liberties. Neither did anybody else. Kelly had learned that the Narcissan Teddybear was the only creature in known space to have developed lovability as a survival mechanism.

"I don't know about you, Kelly, but I feel we erred in bringing that sphere aboard. It's in violation of natural law, and I long ago made a vow never to space with violations of natural law. It gives me a feeling of uneasiness, as when someone aboard ship mentions a certain four-legged animal that oinks and makes bacon. I'm not superstitious, you understand, but it simply isn't done."

"Bert, do you really think that thing's an alien artifact?"

"Why fabricate a thing and bury it in diamond? It smacks of vulgar ostentation. True, it would last longer that way than by doing almost anything else, but what kind of people would have ambitions to perpetuate a work for untold billions of years?"

"Actually," Torwald's voice came from the hatchway, "that's what *I* came to ask *you*." Torwald entered, followed by Achmed, and Torwald picked up Teddy, whereupon the pseudobear began unbuttoning his tunic collar. "Why aren't you studying, kid?"

"We were talking about that thing we found." Kelly was on the defensive. "It seemed more important."

"It is, but that's not why you weren't studying. You were just goofing off, as usual. Let's hear your thoughts, Bert—about the ball, I mean."

"Well, as I see it, Torwald, it could be one of three things: an artifact, a natural object, or an entity."

Achmed started suddenly. "Explain that last one, please. You mean, it could be a sentient being?"

"Possibly. As such, it could still be a natural object *or* an artifact. Remember, intelligent guidance makes

51

a mockery of even our limited knowledge of natural order."

Achmed nodded. "True, Bert, but the fact remains that that thing went into the diamond stratum eons ago."

"So? Stars have been forming and spawning planets for untold millennia. Those planets have been producing intelligent life for a like period. Is it to be wondered at that one of them produced an indestructible object? Or that a life form that is immortal, or nearly so, has evolved? You know that we've all hoped to stumble onto that secret. Sometimes I think that the main reason our species broke into space was to find the secret of immortality."

"I thought we were just going where the money was, Bert."

"You are a man of little scope, Torwald. What is money, after all, except a poor substitute for immortality?" Bert winked at Kelly.

"And you're a sententious old coot!" The quartermaster laughed. "What about you, Achmed?"

"I won't offer any opinions until we have better data. But, I haven't felt so uneasy about a situation since Uncle Abdul let the genie out of the bottle."

Three

He sensed a pursuing malevolence, and a goal, and eons of time so vast that they had no meaning. There was a task of creation and a long, long wait and then there would be a meeting with the Enemy and then—

Kelly woke sweating. The dream had been so alien, yet so real! Kelly wondered if he dared repeat his dream to the others, for fear of being suspected of some psych problem. He decided to try to go back to sleep, but it was no use, so he dressed and set out for the galley. He could at least start breakfast. Anything to keep busy and avoid thought.

He found most of the crew already assembled at the mess table, and they all looked as bad as he felt. Torwald arrived on Kelly's heels.

"Good Lord!" he said, "I've seen brighter faces going into a battle."

"Shut up, Tor," the skipper said. "Now, let's compare notes. Starting with you, Lafayette. What did you see?"

"Damn, Skipper, I don't know, but it sure scared me. There was something chasing me—" he stopped and frowned, searching for words "—no, it wasn't *me,* exactly. It was all happening to something else. Something that wasn't human. And I think it made a planet. I think it made that planet back there." He was becoming more frightened just talking about it.

"Was that all?"

"No, Skipper, there was more, lots more, but that was about all I could begin to understand. Oh, yes, there was something about thinking stars . . ." his voice trailed off in fearful puzzlement.

The skipper looked at Nancy. "How about you?" Nancy related much the same story, cracks beginning to show in her habitual icy poise. It was soon established that the entire crew had seen the same vision. The skipper looked around the table. "Well? Theories? Opinions? Comments?"

"I have a question," Michelle said.

"Let's hear it," the skipper urged.

"How come we're all avoiding looking at that thing?" she pointed at the sphere in the middle of the table. As she said it, everybody turned and looked toward it with a wary horror.

"All right," said the skipper, "this thing is somehow the culprit. Are we all agreed on that?" There were no denials.

"Now comes the big one," said Ham. "Just what is it?"

"May I venture an opinion, Skipper?"

"That's all that any of us can venture just now, Bert. What's yours?"

"If this thing caused that vision, and it can really do what the vision seemed to indicate, then we may be dealing with some kind of god."

"There is only one," said Achmed, quietly.

"I agree," the skipper said. "Although I'll admit that the point is a little academic when dealing with a being that can create a planet out of raw material and wrap it around itself like a blanket. In any case, it's intelligent and extremely powerful."

"Skipper, your mastery of understatement is truly staggering," Torwald commented wryly.

"All right, then, let's hear your thoughts on the matter."

"First off, this may be the first living, intelligent alien humanity has run across. Aside from a few scattered artifacts, we've found no life more intelligent than the average gibbon. So, this is an historic occasion, even if it is kind of spooky."

"Let's not celebrate just yet," the skipper warned. "And second?"

"Second, however powerful this thing is, it was being chased by something even more powerful." This observation caused them to look even more glum for a few minutes.

"That was a long time ago, right, Ham?" Kelly chimed in.

"Time doesn't seem to mean much to these things. Sergei, how old would you estimate Alpha Tau to be?" The Russian shrugged and spread his hands, palms up.

"Two billion years? Three, maybe? Who can tell when the circumstances of its birth are so singular? Numbers like that are meaningless when applied to human perceptions of time, anyway. A few dozen zeros more or less hardly matter."

It is well that you recognize your mental limitations. They all jumped as if they had been stung, several leaping to their feet. If their chairs had not been bolted to the deck, they would have tumbled over backward. The voice had come from within their minds, but there was no doubt as to its origin. They now eyed the sphere with a mixture of fear, awe, and excitement.

"What are you?" The skipper was fighting to keep her voice steady.

A being.

"So we had surmised. We found you during an

excavation. We did not realize that you were intelligent at the time. Do you wish to return?"

No.

That disappointed some of them a bit.

"We are returning to Earth, our home planet, with a cargo of crystal," the skipper said, gaining confidence. "Do you wish to accompany us?"

No.

"I fear that those are your only choices. We are not able to make extensive side trips. Our schedule does not permit it." She was beginning to sweat.

I have a mission. You will help me to accomplish it.

The inward voice was completely uninflected, but the imperative was thrillingly powerful.

"I am in command of this ship, and I refuse."

They all braced themselves.

I would prefer your consent, but you have no choice. I can control this vessel.

"I believe you can do it. But why, with your power, do you need my ship?"

I have exhausted much of my power. I might not be capable of such a journey.

"How far do you need to go?"

To the center of this galaxy.

That gave them all a start. They looked at each other incredulously and all began protesting at once. The skipper silenced them with a glare.

"Look, Sphere, you don't seem to understand. Our species has never traveled so much as a thousandth of that distance. It's debatable whether we could even survive the radiation and stresses at the Center. I might add that we are a short-lived species, by your standards. Even with the Whoopee Drive, we would all die of old age long before we reached the center of the galaxy."

I will change your drive. It is crude even by the standards of mechanical devices. I can protect you from harmful radiation. You will not age significantly during the journey. You must understand that, to me, you are tiny, insignificant specks of life, as inconsiderable to me as the smallest units of living matter on your planet are to you. I who am communicating with you am a minute subdivision of the intellect of the Being you think of as Sphere, detailed for this purpose. The greater part of that intellect is quite unaware of you, and is as oblivious of your function and mine as you are of the cells of your bodies.

You may as well cooperate. You are a primitive and isolated species, obscure even in this little galaxy. At the Center the stars are dense, and you may find many species of planetary beings like yourselves. Surely you will learn things that will be of use to you? It will be the beginning of a new era for your species. If your culture is still based on the exchange of goods, you will find much to your profit.

"Retro me, Satanas," Bert muttered.

Sphere certainly knew how to tempt spacers. Already, they could feel the itch, the intoxicating prospect of getting into unknown space. They would not have been serving in the tramps if they had not had a good deal of the adventurer's spirit in them. The skipper had it worst of all. She looked around at her crew. Even Kelly, who was new to space, was plainly eager to go. Finally she turned to the factor. "Sorry, Sergei. It looks like Minsk gets its crystal a little late."

"So it would seem. We'll renegotiate the contract so that Minsk Mineral gets a percentage of whatever we find. Since we have no choice, we might as well make the best of it."

"An admirable attitude," said Torwald. "And, under the circumstances, the only one possible."

"I don't believe for a minute that we're going to accomplish this without risk," Finn complained. "If we're going to be exploring about unknown places, I'd feel better doing it in a battlewagon instead of in the dear old *Angel*." The others conceded his point.

"I think we could use a Viver." Torwald's suggestion was greeted with astonishment.

The skipper regarded him with suspicion for a moment. The Vivers were the most notorious smugglers in known space. "You've had dealings with Vivers?"

"I worked a few smugglers when berths were hard to come by. I know the code to open negotiations with one of their clan ships. If Sphere will let us stop at New Andorra or one of the other smuggling bases, I can find their location. We could pick up some heavy armament, too."

What are Vivers?

"A subspecies of our race developed before genetic engineering of humans was outlawed in the last century," explained the skipper. "They're adapted to survive under extreme conditions and our own chances of survival would be greatly increased if we had one or more of them among the crew. If you will let us pick up the Viver and some special equipment, we'll willingly help you all we can."

Very well. The time element is insignificant, but our motion must continue to be toward the Core.

"We're agreed, then." The skipper turned to Ham. "Mate, set course for New Andorra, and as soon as we're far enough out, cut in the Whoopee Drive."

That will not be necessary. Indicate the location of this planet on your instruments and I will transfer you there.

"Gertie?" Perplexed, Ham turned to the skipper.

"Do what he says, Ham." Ham left for the bridge, put in course data for New Andorra, and, when nothing further happened, returned to the mess. As he entered, the customary gentle hum of the real-space engines stopped. Achmed jumped up and ran for the engine room with Lafayette in close pursuit.

"Have we stopped?" the skipper asked, looking at Sphere.

No, we are now traveling much more rapidly than the speed your drive is capable of producing. When I

*have absorbed your computer information, I shall
give you equivalent speeds comprehensible to you.*

Achmed returned sheepishly and sat down, bewilderment gleaming in his dark eyes. "Go have a look," he said. "Craziest thing I've ever seen." They all filed down to the engine room. Through the hatch they could see that the room was glowing, as if the air inside had taken on color and light. Streaks of red and yellow chased one another in convoluted patterns around the room, and points of bright green flitted about like tiny insects. There was no sound at all.

"Very pretty," Ham said, trying without much success to sound unperturbed.

When they returned to the mess, Michelle remembered that they hadn't had breakfast yet. Michelle, Kelly, and Torwald got busy, while the others sat silently, bemused expressions on their faces. They were finishing their coffee when the Sphere spoke up again.

We have reached your destination.

By this time, the crew had stopped doubting. The skipper went forward to the bridge to check. Sure enough, Sphere had set them neatly in a parking orbit around New Andorra.

Truro, sole urban center of New Andorra, was a sprawling collection of buildings large and small, many of them warehouses, surrounding a spaceport. Most of the population was transient, mainly smugglers, their customers, and middlemen who did business with both. There were no government and no law, but violence was not all-pervasive. The population saw itself as consisting of peaceful business people. The sole organized body was the Port Authority, which saw to the running and upkeep of the spaceport.

Truro was the largest transshipment point for smugglers in known space. If a buyer wanted drugs, luxury goods, arms—anything that might be illegal, highly taxed, or government-controlled where he came from—Truro was the place to find it. The inhabitants of New Andorra would sell the merchandise there or deliver it for a fee. New Andorra was far enough from the centers of space travel so that most governments never found it worth their while to clean it out. Besides, a fair number of governments did a little clandestine business with the New Andorrans.

Kelly was ready for some time on planet. The novelty of spacing was quickly wearing off, and he had found that confinement in a small ship, seeing the same few faces every day, could dim the strongest enthusiasm for space travel. There was a price, though. Torwald had made him repaint the supply room and machine shop lab before getting any shore time, a job he'd been dodging for weeks. He caught up with the planetside party just as it was about to leave.

"I'm finished," said Kelly.

"I guess we'll have to let you come along," Ham said, wrinkling his nose. "You need airing out. You smell like paint."

"Let's go," said the skipper, taciturn as usual. The captain, Ham, Torwald, and Kelly, composed the arms-buying expedition. The others were off locating supplies for their departments, to be laid in later by the quartermaster. It would be another headache for Kelly, who would be doing most of the work. Torwald took the boy's training seriously and believed in on-the-job instruction.

The *Space Angel*'s port fees were paid before the crew left for the city. They received some strange looks from the approach-control officers, who were puzzled at the way the *Angel* had popped directly from hyper into parking orbit. There were no questions, though. Truro was one port where a spacer was safe from embarrassing inquiries.

Torwald, who was familiar with Truro, took charge of the arms-buying expedition, quickly making inquiries about the best dealer from whom to obtain

arms. He was advised to try a bar called the Gun
Runner. Kelly gawked and rubbernecked as they
walked through the crowded streets. New Andorra
was still a frontier world, and most of the buildings
were of local woods, the streets hard-foamed rather
than paved.

The inhabitants were a colorful mixture—men and
women in spacer garb, merchants in expensive fabrics
and furs, tough-looking types, many of them frankly,
theatrically piratical. Almost everyone was armed. For
that matter, so were Torwald, Ham, and the skipper.
The shops were stuffed with valuable merchandise
at suspiciously low prices. The skipper stopped at a
display window. The wares inside consisted mainly of
delicate sculptures of ethereal lightness, made of pre-
cious metals mounting tiny jewels, unmistakably the
work of the Taliesin art colony.

"Ham, what was the name of that ship they found
in orbit around Ivanhoe with no crew and no cargo?"
The skipper was visibly upset.

"*Ebony Star,* Black Star Line."

"That's the one. *Ebony Star* was carrying a lot of
Taliesin art work. The insurance company published
the manifest in the *Spacer's Newsletter.*" Her face
was bleak. "I don't care much for pirates."

"She was probably hijacked by her own crew," Torwald said. "Officers might have been in on it, too.
It happens often enough, Skipper."

"Not in the Black Star Line. They recruit officers
better than that. I don't like mutineers, either. Come
on, let's go find that bar."

There were few real offices in Truro. Most business
was transacted in bars, and particular bars had become associated with a special trade. The Gun Runner
had a hand-carved wooden sign depicting a human
figure sprinting with a bag on his back. From the
mouth of the bag protruded the barrels of forcebeam
rifles. Inside, the public room was dimly lit, the little
light provided by glow-disks stuck to the massive over-

head beams. The interior was smoky and full of odd smells; the walls were decorated with clusters of edged weapons and obsolete firearms and beamers. The skipper chose a table against a wall, beneath an arrangement of old Space Marine sword-knives. Kelly noticed that nobody had asked his age.

Torwald sauntered over to the bar and ordered a bottle and four glasses. When the barkeep returned with his order, Torwald brought up business.

"Who's selling arms today?"

"Well, now, let's see." He scanned the room. "Ames, over there, the one with the blue braids, sells light infantry weapons, and Yussoupov, back at the corner table, just got a load of heavy artillery. Chung has bombs up to the Devastator class—"

"I just need some medium ship artillery, maybe some light rocket torpedoes."

"Then, you want to see Sturges. He's not in just now, but he usually opens up shop about this time. Have a seat and I'll send him over when he comes in."

"Fine. By the way, would you know if Ortega's still in his old place across the street from the Dead Spacer?"

"Last I heard, he was." The barkeep began eyeing Torwald with a different expression. "But that's no part of town for an honest man." Torwald gave the man a sizable tip and carried the bottle and glasses back to the table. He poured four glasses full of a deadly looking purple liquid.

"Genuine Old Rocket Wash, aged twenty years, or so it says on the label," Torwald proclaimed. Kelly took a hesitant swallow, then tried to keep his eyes from watering as the fluid burned a path down his esophagus and cleared his sinuses.

"Smooth," Ham commented. Kelly tried another swallow, and sure enough, it *was* beginning to taste smooth. They were halfway through the bottle when a tall, portly man stepped up to the table. He was heavily jeweled, and his clothes were of gaudy Sirian crab-silk: a tight-fitting shirt with balloon sleeves, wide trousers stuffed into heavy reptile-hide boots, a vest that didn't quite conceal a laser under the left arm and a dagger or forceblade beneath the right. He bowed slightly, touching his chest with the spread fingers of his right hand, a wide smile separating his mustache from his curly, yellow beard.

"My name is Omar Sturges, and I understand you gentlefolk have business to discuss with me?"

"Captain HaLevy of the *Space Angel*." The skipper stuck out her hand. "This is my mate, Hamilton Sylvester, Quartermaster Torwald Raffen, and Ship's Boy Kelly." They shook hands all around. Torwald noticed that Sturges's palm was hard and calloused, and he could feel metal caps implanted beneath the skin over his knuckles. It would not pay to underestimate this man. The skipper poured him a drink and he took a chair.

"I understand that you deal in ship's arms, Mr. Sturges."

"That is true, Captain. I have singlebeams suitable for small scouts, pulse-lasers from scrapped cruisers, and so on—up to heavy armament for battlewagons. Price includes installation. What are you interested in?"

"We just need some explorer-ship defensive gear," Ham replied. "Can you sell us a six-beam long range cutter on a hex mount? We can mount the hex around the *Angel*'s nose."

"Yes, I have several of those. Anything else?"

"How about a turret-mounted twin depolarizer?"

"No problem."

"And four subnuclear torpedoes, Class M?"

"I have some Class Ks. The Cernunnans bought up all my Class Ms for their little war with Ganpati."

While Ham and the skipper haggled with Sturges over price, Torwald excused himself and beckoned Kelly to follow. They went out and blinked for a few moments in the brilliant light, then set off with Torwald in the lead.

"Stick close by me, Kelly. We're heading for a rough part of town, and the man we're going to see is uncommonly suspicious. If you think somebody's following us, let me know."

Kelly looked about in alarm. The part of town they were in seemed sufficiently rough. He was no stranger to tough neighborhoods; the slums of Earthport were notoriously unruly, but the boy felt a bit out of his depth in a city where almost the whole population was engaged in one criminal undertaking or other. Kelly was reassured by the laser pistol on Torwald's hip, and he knew that the slug pistol was somewhere beneath his friend's vest.

As they walked the surroundings became shabbier and more dilapidated. The people in the streets, instead of swarming indiscriminately, congregated in small clusters on corners and, occasionally, in front of doorways. Richly dressed merchants were no longer to be seen, and the groups Torwald and Kelly passed looked them up and down in casual speculation. The sight of a well-armed spacer seemed not to tempt them, and the loungers, mostly young men, returned to whatever discussion had been interrupted.

Eventually, the two reached a bar with a sign depicting a figure in a spacesuit with a ruptured helmet, floating against a field of stars. Undoubtedly, this was the Dead Spacer. They crossed the street and entered a nondescript warehouse. Torwald signaled Kelly to imitate him, then entered, hands well away from weapons, walking slowly. Kelly followed. Inside, the light was as dim as it had been in the Gun Runner.

Amost immediately a small dark man emerged from behind a pile of boxes. His face was hideously scarred, and he had artificial eyes that gleamed blankly, giving away nothing. He looked the two newcomers over without fear. Shadowy figures were visible among the boxes behind him. Finally, he seemed satisfied.

"Been a long time, Raffen. You look prosperous."

"Not as prosperous as you, Ortega." Torwald turned slowly, surveying the loot that filled the warehouse. "Seems you've picked up some new eyes since I last saw you."

"They gouge eyes for smuggling on Quetzalcoatl. What do you need? Want to get back into the profession? If so, I know a few skippers who could use a good hand like you."

"Thanks, Ortega. I just need some information this time. I'll pay the usual rate. I need the location of the clan ship *K'Tchak*."

"This one safe?" Ortega nodded toward Kelly.

"He's my squire." Kelly wondered at this. He had not realized that he had a status other than ship's boy. But Ortega was answering.

"K'Tchak's in orbit around Donar until end-of-cycle. That leaves you plenty of time. After that, she heads for the Homeworld." Nobody except the Vivers knew where Homeworld lay. Torwald handed the man a stack of metal plates.

"Thanks, Ortega. I'd like to talk over old times, but we have to get back to the ship—urgent assignment. Maybe next trip."

"Torwald," Ortega called just as the two reached the wide wooden doors of the warehouse, "you have enemies here. Some of 'em still remember the *Jonah*. Don't drop your guard before you reach your ship."

"Thanks, Ortega." Torwald turned, reached beneath his vest, and extracted the slug pistol. "You ever use one of these, Kelly?"

"No."

"Remind me to give you lessons sometime. Don't worry about it just now. If we get hit in these streets, it'll be at short range. Just stick that in somebody's belly and pull the trigger. You've got thirty shots. One or two ought to be enough. Shift your sticker to the back of your belt, where you can get at it with either hand."

"But I'm right-handed."

"Suppose the first warning you get that the fun's about to start is a bullet through your right arm?" Kelly stuffed his knife sheath into the crease of his back. The slug pistol went into his belt.

The sky was quickly darkening when they left the warehouse. Truro was located just north of New Andorra's equator, near the sea, so the transition from day to night was brief. The streets were dim, and the lengthening shadows of the buildings formed inky pools across the thoroughfare. Torwald headed for the spaceport, Kelly following a few steps behind, ears cocked for following footsteps. They were not long in coming.

"Tor," Kelly whispered, "I hear two men behind us."

"There's three in front. I'm going to do some talking, but there's no talking our way out of this. Don't go for your gun until I go for mine. You take care of those two behind us." Suddenly the three ahead made their appearance. In the light of a doorway, they appeared to be street thugs of the standard variety— youngish men in gaudy clothes, their dissipated faces wearing arrogant smirks. They looked stupid, unpredictable, and dangerous.

"Just hold it right there." The biggest of the three, a tall man with gold studs decorating his vest, spoke.

"You boys have business with us?" Torwald asked. Behind Kelly, the sounds of the other two ceased. He gave no sign of noticing their presence.

"Just wanted to ask you about your ship," Gold Studs said, scratching his slight paunch. "Thought you could maybe use some crew, times being kind of lean around here."

"Well," Torwald said, "I'll mention it to the skipper, but—" without breaking the cadence of his speech, he drew his laser as Gold Studs' fingers darted beneath his vest. The beam slashed into the thug's side. Simultaneously, Kelly spun and drew his pistol, firing at the nearer of the two men now closing in from behind. He fired again as Torwald's laser burned into the arm of the man on Gold Studs' right. Kelly's second shot, panicky and a little off center, struck his second man in the shoulder, spun him around, and sent him staggering into the dark. The man on Gold Studs' left turned and ran, quickly followed by the man with the rayed arm. From Torwald's last word to the fleeing of the unwounded man, less than four seconds had elapsed.

The sound of the shots and the flash of the laser drew some curious glances through the doors of nearby bars, but they were quickly withdrawn. Torwald and Kelly walked casually away, as if nothing out of the ordinary had happened. From behind them could be heard the sounds of men disputing possession of Gold Studs' pistol.

"Did you know those men?" Kelly was trying unsuccessfully to keep his voice steady.

"Never saw them before. Those were hired men. Hired cheap, too, I imagine. That kind will kill you for a good pair of boots." His voice changed slightly. "You did well, Kelly. I shouldn't have let you get into this, but I won't forget it." Kelly could say nothing.

When they returned to the ship, it was brilliantly lighted, lamps directing beams from all directions as work crews installed the new weaponry.

"Sturges wastes no time, I see," Torwald commented.

From her vantage point on the ramp, the skipper caught sight of their faces as they boarded.

"What's wrong with him?" she asked Torwald, after Kelly boarded. Torwald gave her a brief account of the confrontation, then continued on to the mess, where most of the crew was already gathered and Michelle was administering the age-old nerve tonic from a bottle. Michelle glared at Torwald as he entered. He held out his hands, palms forward, to forestall what he assumed would be her blistering comments.

"My fault," he said. "I shouldn't have taken him

there. But, I never thought I'd still have enemies in this place."

"Damn right it's your fault," the skipper said. "If he'd been hurt, I'd have kicked you off this ship so hard you would've gone into hyper!"

"I'm all right!" Kelly yelled, nettled at their solicitude. "Don't make such a big deal about it. We were attacked and we fought and that's all there is to it."

"Sure," said Ham, "the kid's learning like the rest of us. No harm done, just the removal of a couple of punks that this place can probably spare, and a couple of others put out of action for a while."

"That's all there was to it," said Kelly. "Don't give Torwald a hard time just because of me."

"Then, what *is* bothering you?" Nancy asked quietly.

"Well . . . it's just that, I can't help thinking. A couple more years without finding a ship, and I could've been one of those scum back there. There were plenty like that back in Earthport. Sooner or later, I'd have had to join a gang like that if I wanted to survive. And I'd have probably ended up gunned down in an alleyway, too. So let's just be glad the right side won and leave it at that, okay?" he stared at the skipper.

"Sure, Kelly," she said, after a few moments' hesitation. "Now, go to your cabin and keep out of sight till we leave port." Kelly got up and left.

"Torwald, do you think your former friends will try to get to you or Kelly aboard ship?"

"No chance, Skipper. Nobody here makes trouble within the port. It's neutral territory. Anybody tries to make difficulties inside the port perimeter, all the others will be out to get him."

"You're lucky that's the case," she said. "All right, everybody, we up ship in three hours, as soon as I've had time to check out the newly installed equipment. Torwald, you get the coordinates for the Viver ship?"

"Parking orbit around Donar."

"That's the right direction, anyway. Old Sphere shouldn't kick up any fuss. Okay, everybody, get ready to button up. Next stop is—what's the name of the ship, Torwald?"

"Viver clan ship *K'Tchak*."

Four

It was Kelly's watch on the bridge, and as usual, he was studying. It seemed he was always studying these days. At least, he was studying when he wasn't being worked to exhaustion. It had never occurred to him that spacing would be so much like going to school. But then, he had never before realized the depth of his ignorance. The State schools had been little more than an excuse to keep the younger War orphans and refugees off the streets for a while.

Lost time was being made up for now. Whenever he could be spared from work, he would study chemistry or navigation with Finn, supply and paperwork with Torwald, engineering with Achmed, and Bert seemed able to teach just about anything. Nancy was teaching him communications, but no matter how hard he tried, he couldn't inveigle her into any other line of conversation.

Just now, he was reading up on Vivers. Kelly could find little in the ship's library on the strange creatures.

He asked Torwald, and the older spacer gave him a microfilm monograph, written by none other than one Torwald Raffen, that contained more accurate information than any "official" document about the secretive subspecies.

Kelly learned that in the last century, a few decades after the first interstellar drive was perfected, a group of geneticists got together and decided, after the fashion of scientists, that the human race could stand some improvement. They were going to create the Future Man. It was decided that humans were good mainly for surviving and that the new human race would have to be even better at it in order to be equal to the unknown exigencies of new worlds. It was agreed that the upright, bipedal, digit-handed human form could scarcely be improved upon for generalized capability, but that little improvements could be added here and there, specialties without specialization, as it were. Onto this they grafted a mentality obsessively concerned with survival. The result was the Viver, though it was not quite what they had planned. The fear that Vivers generated in ordinary humans was sufficient to get genetic engineering of humans banned forever. Kelly scratched Teddy's ears and pondered that. The pseudobear had become a close friend, for it seemed to be the only life form on board that didn't give him orders, chew him out, or think up unpleasant jobs for him to perform.

The typical Viver, Kelly read, was between six and seven feet tall and covered with horny, articulated plates of chitin that roughly followed the lines of human musculature. The hands were human in design but much larger, the knuckles covered with a spiked band of bone. The fingertips were equipped with inch-long retractile claws that did not interfere with ordinary use of the fingers when sheathed. Elbows and knees were heavily knobbed and bore large spikes. The feet had no toes, the foot being equipped with a club of bone and chitin where the toes should be. At the back of the leg, just below the calf, was a protrusion somewhat like a horse's fetlock that concealed a seven-inch razor-sharp spur, perhaps the deadliest of the Viver's natural weapons.

The head, set on a long flexible neck, was the least human feature of a Viver. The eyes were huge, taking up most of the skull's interior. They were covered with a transparent plate and could swivel independently of one another. There were several, smaller apertures around the skull for the eyes to peer through. The beings had no true teeth, just serrated chitin.

Internally, Vivers differed even more radically from the human parent stock. The brain was distributed throughout the body in tiny nodes, and the heart was likewise decentralized, being a series of small pumps distributed throughout the circulatory system. Practically the only way to kill a Viver was to cut him up into very small pieces. All parts, including brain tissue, were regenerative. It had been speculated that if a Viver were split in two down the middle, two complete Vivers would be the eventual result. So far no one had had the nerve to try that particular experiment.

Psychologically, all else was subordinate to the survival imperative. A Viver concerned himself with the survival of his race, his clan, his family, and himself. There were no political loyalties, only biological ones. They were smugglers because they had no respect whatever for ordinary human laws. They would have made invincible soldiers, but they saw war as a threat to their survival and studiously ignored conflicts between ordinary humans.

However, there was one exception. Young Vivers, before being judged fit to reproduce, had to undergo a period of exile during which they were expected to take part in wars and other adventures of a violent sort. It was for this last reason that the *Space Angel* was calling upon the good ship *K'Tchak*.

The Viver ship resembled a collection of buildings held together with tubes and braces, and, essentially, that was what it was. Built in space, it was never intended to land. The craft had to be big, for it contained almost all of the clan K'Tchak, and additions were made as the clan expanded. Despite their horrible tempers, Vivers liked the company of their own kind and ran to large families. It was all part of their obsession with survival.

As she approached, the *Angel* had about a fleet's worth of armament trained on her. This was not because of her new weaponry; lifeboats received the same treatment from a Viver clan ship. Torwald gave a few passwords over the ship-to-ship and obtained grudging permission to go aboard, alone. As a security precaution, the skipper insisted that Torwald carry a scanner giving full aural and visual communication with those aboard the *Angel*. The Vivers did not object to the procedure; Vivers understood all about security precautions.

The remainder of the *Space Angel*'s crew gathered on the bridge to monitor the proceedings. Torwald was met at the lock by a dozen or so heavily armed Vivers who escorted him down a dreary corridor to an unmarked cubicle that contained no furnishings but a desk. Aboard a Viver ship, all was bare, functional, Spartan. Behind the desk sat a Viver whose high rank was plain from the jeweled handles of his weapons. Weapon decoration was the high point of Viver aesthetics. The official wasted no time on introductions.

"What business have you with the glorious K'Tchak?"

"Our mission is one of extreme danger. If you have one or two young people who are due for their adulthood ritual, it would be a good test for them."

"You do well for yourselves to ask. Soft people like you are not well suited to strenuous tasks. Yes, we have two such. Their names are K'Stin and B'Shant.

73

They are of the best families. The glory of their bodies shines even among Vivers. Among you pulpy persons, their beauty and durability shall be as diamonds among mushrooms."

"I am sure that they are as hard to kill as a pack of ship rats," Torwald replied courteously. "Would they like to come with us?"

"Who cares what they want?" the official snorted. "It is time for them to go, so they go. If they do not come back, they will have failed. Return to your ship now. The sight of their degenerate parent stock may corrupt our young. The two shall be sent to you shortly."

The crew met Torwald upon his return to the *Angel,* eager to know what to expect.

"The Vivers must be training diplomats," Torwald said. "I never met one before who was so suave and urbane."

"All right," said the skipper, "let's have it. What are we in for? I've never shipped with a Viver, and I don't think anyone else here has, either."

"First of all, folks, you'll find them a bit overbearing. The Vivers have the utmost contempt for us standard-variety humans. In fact, they're already developing a mythology in which they weren't derived from human stock at all. The idea is as repugnant to them as the theory of the animal origin of humanity was to the Victorians. Also, they react to the slightest threat with devastating violence, so don't step on their, ah, well, they don't have toes, but don't step on *anything*.

"Michelle, you won't have to worry about doctoring them because they don't get sick, and anything that gets chopped off grows back. They can metabolize just about anything, so you can feed them fertilizer from Hydroponics if you like."

"What's their language?" Nancy asked.

"The one they use among themselves is secret, but they're accomplished linguists. Their voice boxes can reproduce almost any sound, and they can speak and hear well into the super- and subsonics."

"Can we trust them?" Ham asked, lighting up a cigar.

"As long as they don't think we're deliberately trying to kill them. They're fantastically suspicious, so we'd better not order them to take any risks that we're not taking, too. Their test is supposed to be dangerous, or it would be meaningless. It's only during this period that any Viver will risk his existence at the orders of a non-Viver."

"Where are you going to billet them?" the skipper asked.

"They'll have to have their own quarters, or else the situation would be too volatile. Luckily, their tastes are pretty simple, so I've decided to put them in the cleaning-equipment room just aft of the hold. I've already moved the equipment to the supply room."

Just then the main lock buzzer announced the arrival of the newcomers, and the skipper cycled the lock open for their new shipmates. The first one through was a seven-footer, followed by a companion about half a foot shorter.

"I am K'Stin," said the taller, "son of K'Tok, who is commander of the *Avenger*, grandson of K'Din, who slew thousands in the battle off Wotan, great-grandson of K'Tang, who built the first great clan ship, and so on back to K'Tchak, founder of the clan. This," he jerked a taloned thumb over his shoulder at the shorter one, "is B'Shant, whose ancestry is not quite as illustrious as mine, but is still quite respectable. He is my ninety-second cousin by seven lines of parallel descent and forty-four marriage ties, with a number of ambiguous familial tangencies. I am sure that you soft and depraved persons have no appreciation of such things, but you may rejoice in our protective presence."

"Pleased to meet you," the skipper said. "Now, I

notice that you two are dripping with weapons, which is fine with me, since most of your duties will involve using them. However, we're now in space, so please hand over your lightbeam and high-velocity projectile weapons, to be put in the ship's arms locker."

Both Vivers drew into defensive postures.

"Nonsense!" shouted K'Stin. "Abandon weapons in the presence of strangers? I make scornful and insulting noises at you! I am struck with mirth at the very idea."

Trouble already. Michelle stepped in diplomatically to smooth things over. "Now, gentlemen, surely you can't anticipate any threat from our feeble selves? I am sure that the eleven of us, armed or unarmed, could be no match for two of the glorious K'Tchak, or even for one. You must understand our anxiety about any device aboard ship that might damage the hull. Even a slight drop in our oxygen level can kill us, though it would be but a slight discomfort to you."

"We never have accidents with weapons," K'Stin said. "You have nothing to fear."

"True, of course, but there is always the possibility of a mechanical malfunction. Besides, the whole point of this exercise, for you, is the endurance of hardship and danger. Suppose you begin by learning to get along without those power weapons?"

With poor grace they gave the skipper their powered arms, dipping into their bags until she had about a half-dozen from each. This did not leave them exactly unarmed. The deck was now littered with swords, clubs, collapsible spears, bows, slings, garrotes and a variety of other lethal hardware. The skipper dubiously eyed a bandolier of grenades K'Stin had handed her. "You sure that's all?" she asked.

"They would not let us come heavily armed," K'Stin assured her. "If we need more powerful arms, we must make them. Only the bare essentials are allowed on the manhood test."

"Show them their quarters, Kelly," the skipper said. "We leave orbit in twenty minutes. K'Stin, you and B'Shant join us in the mess after you've stowed your gear and we'll fill you in on the mission." Turning to go, she muttered *sotto voce,* "Hah! As if I knew."

"Come along," Torwald urged politely, as he and Kelly ushered the Vivers into the companionway and toward the cleaning-equipment room. Kelly opened the hatch to their quarters and showed the pair inside. He and Torwald had rigged two oversized bunks from tube steel and webbing and added a few shelves made from scrap. The room looked like a monk's cell.

"Will this suit you?" asked Torwald.

"I don't know," K'Stin ventured. "I've never had much taste for luxury."

"Stick with us and we'll make a voluptuary out of you yet."

"Your kinsman doesn't talk much," Kelly observed.

"Of course not. B'Shant is my subordinate since I tore his leg off in the Adolescent Wrestling Rite." K'Stin continued, warming to the subject: "I was also champion in the Grand Post-Adolescent Free-For-All, which is fought with knives and clubs. I received highest marks in dismemberment and marksmanship throughout boyhood. None was better than I at hand weapons—with the exception of K'Tork, who was a little better with the heavy bill hook."

When the Vivers had stowed their belongings, mostly lethal, on the shelves, Torwald conducted them to the mess.

K'Stin looked as puzzled as a Viver can look when he entered. The skipper and Ham were seated at the table, and Sphere occupied its usual place of honor as centerpiece.

"When do we jump to hyper?" K'Stin asked, directing his question at the skipper.

"We already have."

"Foolishness! Impossibility! The effects of interstellar jump are disturbing even to such magnificent creatures as us. Surely I would have noticed. Why do you deceive us?"

"That thing"—the skipper pointed at Sphere—"is a living, unbelievably powerful entity. It possesses the secret of a far more efficient FTL drive that doesn't have the side effects of the Whoopee Drive. It's taking us to the center of the galaxy—"

Both Vivers jumped up, hands on their knives. "This is insane!" B'Shant yelled, the first words he had spoken since coming aboard.

K'Stin swatted him backhanded across the face for daring to speak first. The blow would have torn an ordinary man's head off. "Silence! I say what is insane around here! And I say this is insane!"

It is quite true.

The Vivers froze for a moment, then K'Stin gobbled out a phrase in a language none of the standard humans understood. Kelly felt a twinge in his ears; apparently some of the words went into the supersonic. Sphere replied in what sounded like the same tongue. The Vivers slowly resumed their seats.

"It knows the Secret Tongue," K'Stin said. "Only a Viver should know that, and that thing is no Viver. How old is it?" A typical Viver question.

My age is so great that it could not be encompassed in your mathematics. I was old when your galaxy was a cloud of dust and gas.

"I think he exaggerates," K'Stin announced loudly. "Still, to have such knowledge is indicative of estimable longevity. I must refuse this mission, however. The test calls for severe danger, not suicide."

"First off," said Ham, "we can't go back. Old Sphere, there, has complete control of the ship's drive, and it won't tolerate movement that isn't toward the center of the galaxy. But consider a moment: If we complete this mission, whatever that may be, and by some chance return, think what we'll have learned. Think what secrets we'll have discovered and brought back. K'Stin, would you want us standard humans to have a monopoly on such knowledge?" The mate was learning quickly how to talk to Vivers.

"Knowledge is strength," the Viver mused, nodding. "One can never have too much strength. Also, might we not discover threats at the Center which we Vivers must encounter someday? It would likewise be desirable to learn more about this Sphere thing. There may be more of them, and it does seem to possess an admirable durability. Very well, we go with you willingly. The Grand Council of the Homeworld must receive word of this at all costs. Sphere, what is your mission at the Center?"

Nothing that need concern you. Merely bear in mind that your return home depends upon your success in delivering me to my destination.

"Nancy, how much of the galaxy has been explored by humans?" Kelly asked the question as he helped the Communications officer program her computer. It was the question nagging all of them, now that they had time to reflect. Their adventure became real as they spent long weeks in hyper, longer than any of them had ever spent outside of real space.

"Not much," said Nancy. For several days, Kelly had been able to elicit short sentences from her in addition to instructions in communications and computer handling. "I've read that if you blew up a picture of the galaxy to the size of a sports stadium, the area traversed by humans would be about the size of a peanut."

"And we're about to go millions of times farther than anyone's gone before. I wonder where we are now."

"When you're in hyper, you're not exactly anywhere. Hasn't Finn been giving you lessons in hyperspatial geometry and navigation?"

"Sure, but I really don't understand much. The State schools didn't emphasize the finer points of education, you know." Without his wanting it, Kelly's voice had taken on an edge of bitterness and even a little envy.

"I couldn't read until I was thirteen, Kelly." Nancy was staring at him coolly.

"That's hard to believe."

"My parents were rice farmers on Li Po who worked the Warlord's estate as serfs. When the Commandos unsuccessfully raided to capture the Warlord, I was evacuated with some other children to a refugee ship with the armada. We were lucky. We missed the invasion.

"Me and my big mouth," said Kelly, shamefaced. He had always felt sorry for himself because he had no parents. Now he realized that Nancy didn't even have a *planet!* "How did you get to be a Communications officer?"

"I was sent to a refugee camp on Baldur. One day the *Angel* landed at our field, delivering food on a government contract. I got myself on the work detail carrying empty grain sacks back to the hold. When the others left, I buried myself in the sacks and waited. When I figured we were far enough away from Baldur that the *Space Angel* wouldn't return, I revealed myself. Luckily, I'd fallen in with a good tramp and not one of the line ships that goes by the book.

"They put me to work as ship's girl, the same job you have now. Luckily, Bert's an exschoolteacher, and I learned the basics pretty quickly. The old comm officer took me on as his apprentice, and by the time he was ready to retire a couple of years ago, I had my papers and just stepped into the position. I've been lucky, I guess."

Torwald's head appeared in the hatch. "Nancy, can you spare me your assistant, there, for a while?"

"Sure, Tor. We're about finished here, anyway." Kelly followed Torwald to the supply room. He knew that Torwald had been taking everybody's measurements for body armor. While inventorying the stores, Torwald and Kelly had found sheets of hardened ceramic fiber, and Torwald had decided to make armor for everyone since it seemed likely that they would be in some decidedly hostile surroundings, if not actual combat. He and K'Stin had improvised shaping dies with which the heated ceramic could be pressed into shape, then rehardened. Kelly went through the supply room and into the machine shop, where the floor was littered with pieces of armor.

"Fashion-show time," Torwald announced. "This is your suit, so let's see if it fits. First, the legs." Each was made in one piece, to snap around leg and thigh, and was held shut by its own springiness. The knees were much more complex and required exact fitting for easy movement. The arm pieces were similar. Breast-and-back plates were made in several overlapping pieces for mobility. When the boy was fully fitted, Torwald had him jump, squat, lie down, and get up until he was satisfied that the armor was properly fitted. Kelly admired himself in the supply room mirror. He looked like a Space Marine recruiting poster.

"Where did you learn to make this stuff?" Kelly asked, admiring the sleek lines and gleaming black surface.

"During the War I had to convalesce for six months after copping a wound, so they put me to work in the armory of a Marine troopship. With your helmet on and your visor shut, you'll be almost invulnerable in that . . . Okay, kid, it fits. You can take it off."

"Torwald, what do you think about this crazy trip we're on?"

"Think? Well, mostly I try not to think about it at all. Because, if I have to think about it, here's the inescapable conclusion: Nobody knows the nature of the Center, but it's believed that the stresses, radiation, and even the natural processes differ so radically from what pertains in our little bailiwick out toward the Rim that exploration might prove impossible, even if we could come up with a drive that could make the trip in less than ten generations. Now, I'm going to traverse almost a full radius of the galaxy, and not on a huge, lavish exploration vessel. Instead, I'm going in a beat-up, superannuated tramp freighter armed with a couple of popguns, navigated by a sapient football, and crewed by kids and rejects."

"Is it really that bad?" asked Kelly.

"Just about. Well, Drake's *Golden Hind* was a miserable little cockleshell displacing a hundred and twenty tons, and he sailed it clean around the world and took a Spanish treasure ship, to boot. Maybe we'll be as lucky. Maybe."

A thump at the hatch announced a visitor—two visitors, in fact: Bert and Finn. Bert opened the conversation.

"Things have been going a bit fast until now, and a certain trepidation sets in. Is that thing really going to take us where it says it will? If so, can we survive the trip? Having accomplished its purpose, will it really send us back? I, for one, have no ambition to crew on the *Flying Dutchman* of the inner galaxy."

"Look at it this way," Finn said. "It's like being in the Navy again. We go where we're sent because Someone In Charge finds it meet that we should do so. The choice has been taken out of our hands."

"We've always got old Sphere, Finn. Bert's said that its powers are nearly godlike. Maybe it really can protect us."

"I've revised my estimate, Kelly. It might have been godlike at one time, but no longer. It needs a ship to travel in, doesn't it? If it's reduced to reliance on mechanical devices for movement, maybe its other powers are similarly weakened."

"And," Finn continued, "it regards us with about the same esteem that we accord to amoebae. It might discard us at any time should we prove no longer useful."

"Don't talk like that where the Vivers can hear you," Torwald said. "Talk like that stirs up their survival instincts. They might try to cycle us through the airlock and take the ship back themselves, not that they'd ever be able to navigate back from wherever Sphere's got us now."

"Do you think bringing those two along was such a good idea?" Finn asked. "They're ill-mannered and volatile, and whereas they may be survival specialists compared to us, their chances against what we're likely to encounter at the Center are laughably low."

"They're no guarantee of survival," Torwald admitted. "But, they may give us an edge. Wait till you see them in action." A voice from the intercom interrupted the conversation.

"Kelly, coffee to the bridge." Kelly took a quick leave of the others in the supply room, dashed across the companionway into the galley, drew a pitcher of coffee from the dispenser, then ran forward to the bridge up the companionway between Communications and Navigation. As he entered, he found the skipper in her customary chair, Bert in the mate's chair next to her, and K'Stin standing between them. One of the Viver's eyes darted around to a rear aperture to see who was behind him, and his leg spurs unsheathed about an inch in anticipation of defense. It was an unnerving habit that Kelly had noticed before.

"Just me, K'Stin. Here's the coffee, Skipper. How do the instruments read?"

"Nothing that makes any sense. I've just been familiarizing K'Stin with the controls."

"Yes. Since you will all probably be killed, B'Shant and I must know how to pilot this vessel home."

Kelly leaned over the skipper's shoulder and looked at the panel. By now he had had some basic instruction in the ship's controls, but he had never seen the dials and screens behaving like this. Two screens were blank, but three others glowed nonsensically with a multitude of colors.

"Whatever kind of hyperspace we're in," the skipper continued, "it's not the one that the Whoopee Drive takes us into. Instruments don't act like this during a standard jump. Sphere's been soaking up the computer's memory banks for the last couple of hours. Pretty soon it's going to know all of human history and most of human knowledge." She fiddled and fumed for a while, then lit up one of her cigars.

"Kelly," she said, finally, "when you go back, tell Torwald to start setting up some kind of survival training system. We've got lots of time on our hands and little to do. You younger hands haven't had training like that and the rest of us are rusty. It'll give us something to do, and maybe leave us a little better prepared for what's ahead."

From somewhere, Torwald unearthed a stack of Navy manuals, and he, Ham and Bert put together classes in escape and evasion, camouflage, ballistics, field medical procedure, basic scavenger mechanics, and dozens of other subjects. The course served to keep them mentally active and, as Torwald explained, they cultivated a receptive frame of mind—something always valuable when one hasn't the first idea of what will happen next. The extra work also helped keep the crew from getting on each other's nerves. At best the *Space Angel*'s complement was used to a freighter's short jumps; the crew had not been chosen to function smoothly through long periods of tedium, as had the crews of big explorer ships.

For weapons training, Torwald rigged dummy pistols and beam rifles from scrap metal and plastic, with functioning sights and triggers that activated harmless light beams. To keep the crew in shape while confined to the ship's cramped area, he had the younger crew members carry heavy packs the length of the ship at a dead run along the companionways dozens of times daily. The Vivers regarded these exercises with tolerant amusement.

One day, when Torwald was giving Kelly unarmed —and unrequested—combat instruction, Sphere at last spoke up.

We are now in real space.

Kelly beat Torwald through the door by two paces and they both dashed for Finn's navigation bubble, closely followed by the rest of the crew. Beneath the clear blister, they stood speechless, seeing the stars as men had never seen them before; even the Vivers seemed awed.

Single stars could be seen, double stars, triples, stars in clusters of hundreds and of thousands. Stars of every color were visible: red giants glowed big as the moon on a clear summer night, pinpoint blue-white dwarfs, so bright it was painful to look at them, so many stars that it was as bright as daylight inside the bubble. And everywhere, in clouds and curtains and delicate veils, were nebulae, gas clouds, dust clouds, and the ghostly remnants of long-ago novas, shimmering like silken webs, multicolored gauzes so vaporous that it seemed impossible that they could be real.

"If we never make it back," Michelle whispered to Torwald, "it was worth it to see this."

"Sphere," said the skipper, after another lengthy silence, "how far are we from the Center?"

About 90 percent of the distance is behind us now. You are looking back the way we have come, toward the Rim. Now, I will show you the Center.

The ship rotated slowly, the stars seeming to move overhead, and the center of the galaxy hove over the edge of the horizon formed by the ship's side like a sunrise, only this "sun" was composed of billions of stars and was so bright that the bubble's filters cut in immediately. Even fully filtered, the Center was impossible to look at directly.

Nancy finally put what they were all feeling into words, "It's the Face of God," she said, her voice trem-

bling and her composure for the first time thoroughly
shaken. "The Face of God, from Dante's *Paradiso!*"

"Thank you, Nancy," said the skipper. "That's how
I'll put it down in the log. I wonder how Dante ever
got out here to see this?"

"What now, Sphere?" Ham asked when they were
all once again assembled in the mess, their nerves beginning to calm down a bit. Their brains were beginning to chop the experience into digestible chunks that
could be stored away without causing any damage.

*We shall reconnoitre, taking short hops, perhaps
contacting intelligences upon a number of planets.*

"To learn what, Sphere?" The skipper was becoming impatient. "We still don't have the slightest idea
what we're supposed to be looking for, or what we're
supposed to do when we find it. Will you kindly en-
lighten us?"

*You are to look for news, information, intelligence.
What you do when you have collected this intelligence
I shall tell you at that time.*

"News about what, Sphere?" Ham asked.

About the Core Star.

Silence claimed them for a moment as they thought
that one over. They were trying to remember a detail
from the dream they had all had when Sphere first
came aboard, but no one could recall it with any
clarity.

"All right, what's the Core Star?" The skipper's
anger was becoming more apparent in her voice.

*A phenomenon found at the center of most galaxies
of any magnitude, the star which coalesced at the center of the galaxy when that galaxy first formed. Beyond that mass of stars you saw as the center of this
galaxy, which you termed the Face of God, is a wide
band of empty space, bare of all save wayward clouds
of dust and gas. At its center is the Core Star, a star
a billion times as large as the other largest stars in the
galaxy.*

After taking a few moments to digest that concept, Finn spoke up. "Why doesn't it collapse from the weight of its own mass?"

The rules of physics and the laws of nature with which you are familiar are limited phenomena that pertain only to a narrow spectrum of reality in that tiny zone of the rim of this galaxy you inhabit. They apply considerably less in this zone near the Center and not at all within the Core Star. Within that mass, space, time, reality, take on entirely different meanings. Your minds cannot comprehend it. Even your system of mathematics does not apply. It is as if, within the Core Star, two plus two equals eighty-seven, but that is a simple and misleading example. Just as likely, and more to the point, two plus two equals green. Law exists, but it is not your law.

"If the Core Star is so incomprehensible, how can we gather information about it?" the skipper asked.

You need merely find out what has been occurring within the empty space between the last stars and the Core Star over the last billion or so years.

"I hope you don't want a detailed report," Bert said.

A random sampling will do.

Irony was wasted on Sphere.

"Right, then, down to business," said the skipper. "If we're going to get any information, it'll have to be on Earth-type worlds circling Type G suns. You've had our computer's information, so I presume you can find us such worlds?"

"We, on the other hand, are not so limited," K'Stin said to Sphere. "We Vivers can stand gravity that would crush these puny ones. We can breathe air of a thinness that would collapse their lungs, or water that would drown them. Our chitin is impervious to radiation, which would fry their innards, and our beauty would delight the eyes of any discerning races we might meet, while their ugliness would certainly blight the sensibilities of any such."

"That's okay with me," said Finn. "I'd just as soon they took all the risks, anyway."

Enough of this. Here where the stars are so dense there is no need to explore worlds that are only marginally inhabitable by your kind. Thousands exist like your Earth, and will have developed life analogous to your kind or have been colonized by such.

"Well, when do we start?" asked the skipper.

We have. I have jumped to hyper and we are now within a stellar system around a Type G star that is part of a cluster of many thousands of stars. With the primaries in such proximity, the chances of any favorable planet being inhabited are quite high.

They cruised the system but found no planet duplicating Earth's gravity and atmosphere closely enough. They jumped to another system within the same stellar cluster, but had no better luck. Sphere decided to try for a location closer to the Center.

Five

"**W**hat's the breaking strength of one-ply armor cloth?" Torwald barked at Lafayette.

"Uh, two and one-quarter tons per square centimeter."

Then Torwald pointed to Nancy. "What are the symptoms of fat starvation?"

"Weakness, debilitation, diarrhea, inability to maintain body temperature." Her answer came, as always, without hesitation.

"What's the maximum air speed of our AC fully loaded?" He pointed to Kelly.

"Four hundred kilometers per hour at sea level," said Kelly promptly.

"Only on Earth, dummy!" Torwald said in exasperation. "How many times do I have to tell you not to rely so heavily on manuals? They're always written for a particular set of conditions. In a different gravity and a different air pressure, you have to compute weight, power, and wind resistance. Then you take a guess." He threw up his hands in dramatic supplication of the powers that had sent him such an inept student. Kelly did a slow burn. It wasn't just that he made such mistakes; it was that Torwald always made such a production over them. Nancy never seemed to make mistakes, and when Lafayette made one, he always got off with a simple correction. Torwald's attitude was blatant favoritism in Kelly's view.

The survival classes occupied much of their time now. By ship's time, they had been under hyper for at least nine months. Everything that could possibly be set in order on the ship had long since been completed and the crew was left with little to do. Michelle was predicting serious incidents within a month if some extraship activity didn't break the monotony.

"All right, everybody, up to the navigation bubble!" The skipper's voice rasped excitedly over the intercom. Everyone dropped what he was doing and sprinted toward Navigation. Torwald, Kelly, Nancy, Lafayette, and Michelle all tried to crowd through the hatch at once.

"You look like a bunch of liner passengers on their first lifeboat drill," the skipper commented. "Ain't it great running a tight, disciplined ship, Ham?"

"What's up?" Torwald asked, ignoring the skipper's comments.

"We've got something on the proximity detector. Scan says it's big but artificial—and it's irregular in shape. We're closing on it now. We should have eyeball contact in a few minutes. If it's a ship, then they build big around these parts. This thing's about a hundred kilometers long."

Several minutes later a speck of matter appeared past the nose of the ship, barely visible against the blaze of stars. It loomed quickly larger as the *Angel* decelerated, until it bulked as big as a medium-sized asteroid. But it wasn't a ship, as Michelle had suggested—it was two ships, one roughly platter-shaped, a long, flattish oval, covered with spires and twisted towers, the other a stubby spindle, as if two cones were joined at the base. In some ancient battle or accident these two had collided, the spindle driven through so forcefully that an apex protruded at least a kilometer past the far side of the oval ship. Against the background of the dense star field they were a dark malignancy, their surfaces glinting metallically with reflected starlight. No lights were visible.

"Are they showing any lights we can't see?" Torwald asked.

"Nothing that registers on our instruments," the skipper answered. "Life-scan system seems confused, but in this sector who can tell?" She scanned the improbable ships. "Lord! Look at the size of those things. I don't think the mass of all the ships I've seen could make two that size."

Information may be stored within the instruments aboard those ships. You will board them, taking me with you. My range of power is extremely limited, now.

"The spindle seems to have sustained the least damage to the exterior," said the skipper. "We'll try that one first. Everybody suit up except Bert and Michelle. He and I'll man the bridge while the rest of you check out those vessels. As soon as two of you get tired, we'll relieve you. Ham, you're in charge. I suggest you divide into two teams to save time."

"Right, Gertie. Tor, get some tools from supply: prybars and shortbeams, at least. I doubt that any gravity's functioning in there, so axes will be useless. I'll hand out weapons. Probably no life aboard, but why take chances?"

Within a few minutes they were standing in the lock, bristling with equipment and bulking apishly large in their armored suits. The Vivers wore only their small helmets and the light space coveralls they used to avoid losing too much body moisture. For the first time, Kelly experienced the stomach-dropping sensation of no-grav when the field was shut off as the outer hatch cycled open. One by one, Vivers first, the crew drifted out toward man's first contact with an alien spacecraft.

Close up, the sheer size of the things simply wasn't appreciable. The skipper had parked the *Angel* close to what looked like an airlock, and the landing party could see only the lock and two or three acres of surface around it. The curvature of the spindle's sides obscured all the rest. The surface seemed to be of some bronzy dark metal. The alien ship had enough mass to generate a weak gravity, so the boarders were able to drift to a slow, feet-first landing against the craft.

Sergei, on hands and knees, immediately began to make some tests on the metal with a thick meter-long tube while the others made their way toward the hatch, a circle of metal about ten meters wide, with no visible hinge and no indication of how it might be opened.

"Not even a doorbell," Michelle observed.

"Okay," said Ham, "start earning your pay, people. Let's have some bright ideas."

"I brought some explosive," K'Stin said. "I designed the charge myself. It might make a hole big enough for us to squeeze through."

"Let's not use explosives until we've exhausted all other possibilities. Sergei, what do you make of it?"

"The hull alloy seems metallic, Ham, but it's an alloy containing several elements that aren't on our table, and it doesn't react with any acid in my kit even though it contains a high percentage of copper."

Place me on the hatch.

Nancy stepped forward and set Sphere down on the hatch, near the seam where it joined the hull. Slowly, Sphere began to roll around the circumference of the hatch. Finally, its motion ceased and the spacesuited figures felt a faint vibration through the soles of their boots. Torwald signaled for the others to kneel and put their helmets against the metal of the hull. Faintly, they could hear clicks, groans, and whir- rings from inside. Sphere rolled off the hatch just as it began to move.

Very gradually, the hatch sank into the hull. When it had retracted about a meter, the metal mass began to move sideways and a crescent-shaped gap gradu- ally widened into a full circle.

"Gertie, you see that?"

"I sure do, Ham. What can you see inside?"

Little was visible in the light from their helmet- torches, just a room about the size of the *Angel*'s hold, with six barn-door-sized hatches leading off it. On the walls were pipes or conduits, and metal boxes that might have contained controls or equipment.

"Doesn't look very alien," Ham commented.

"No more so than a loading dock on one of the bigger space stations," said Michelle.

"On such a functional level," Bert mused from the ship, "one might expect little deviation from one cul- ture to another. I'll bet it's not so familiar inside, though."

"First in!" shouted Ham. "Volunteers?"

Kelly began to step forward, but Torwald yanked him back, hard.

"First lesson, me boy," said Finn. "Avoid the word 'volunteer' as if it were the Arcturan Blight. Ham, as ranking officer, I think that you should have the honor. After all, think of the glory, first Earthman to enter an alien spacecraft and all."

"Now, just a minute, one of us has to be in charge of things, to be observing in case the first one down the hatch gets gobbled up by alien space bugs—"

"Ham!" the skipper barked. "Jump into that hole and be quick about it."

"Aye, aye, Gertie." Ham disappeared into the well.

"See anything?" Michelle asked after a few sec- onds.

"Just what we saw from up top, except from a different angle. Come on down." They followed, not without trepidation.

The interior of the room seemed made of the same bronzy material as the hull. The transparent circular plates in the walls might have been lights. Ham stepped to one of the boxes and opened a lid. Inside were several small stubby levers, with no labels or lettering that they could detect. There was one such box to each hatch.

"What next, Sphere?" asked Ham.

I am making an examination. When a hatch opens, enter and proceed by the easiest route. I shall tell you if I wish a change of direction.

As slowly as it had opened, the hatch overhead closed. There was an inrush of air.

"Gertie, can you hear me? Are we still on visual?"

"I hear you, Ham. All your cameras are recording perfectly. Whatever that metal is, it's not very dense. Proceed as seems proper and let's hope that football can get you all out safely."

No sooner had this benediction been delivered than one of the hatches opened. Through it, they could see a corridor stretching at least a kilometer. They could see that much because, incredibly, the ancient lighting system was beginning to function. A dim bluish light was emanating from more of the circular plates set along the walls.

"What's the atmosphere reading, Michelle?" asked Ham.

"It's mostly Argon, Ham," she said. "And this light would be a lot brighter if we could see infrared."

"Argon!" Ham sounded flabbergasted. "D'you think the people who built this ship could have metabolized such a stable gas?"

"Maybe it was injected as a preservative," Bert said. "That could explain why the ship's interior is so well preserved. An inert gas like that won't react with anything. It'd serve to keep the ship preserved over a long voyage."

94

"Well, maybe," Ham said. "Let's just wait until we have more data before we draw any conclusions."

A weak gravity field began to cut in, and things began to take on a more definite "up" and "down" orientation. The deck was about twenty meters wide, its surface corrugated and rather soft. The walls curved inward to form a perfect semicircular arch, giving the corridor the appearance of a tunnel. Torwald stepped over to examine one of the lighting plates, but he could find no central lighting element; the light appeared to originate in the plate itself.

"All right, let's go," said Ham, proceeding down the corridor. The others followed, using the peculiar, stiff-kneed, gliding hop that was the best means of locomotion in a low-gravity environment. They covered more than ten kilometers of corridor without finding any breaks in wall or deck.

"What's our orientation relative to the rest of the ship?" asked Sergei.

"Near as I can figure," Finn said, "we're heading straight down the middle of the spindle, and we've traversed about one-third of its length."

Approximately correct.

"Hey!" yelled Kelly, who had gotten a few meters ahead of the rest, "I see something a ways down there. It looks like a hatch."

They sped forward to see what Kelly had spotted. About a hundred meters farther on was another circular hatch, this one in the deck. Placed low on the wall near by, a circular plate protruded about twenty millimeters above the surface.

"Whoever they were, they were fond of circles and sections of circles," Nancy remarked.

"That thing on the wall looks like a pressure plate," Ham said. "Tor, give it a whack and let's see what happens."

Torwald placed his foot against the plate and gingerly pushed it inward. It sank flush with the wall, then slowly reemerged as he removed his foot. Gradually, the floor hatch slid aside, revealing a well about ten meters deep. About five meters beyond the well was a deck with the same kind of corrugated surface as that of the corridor. A spiral ramp about a meter wide ran around the periphery of the cylindrical well, continued beyond the end of the ramp, and fell free-standing to the deck below.

"If the ramp was their access to the deck below," said Nancy, "then they couldn't have been more than a meter high. Look how close together the levels of the ramp are."

"They probably weren't very quick, either," said Achmed. "Everything we've seen move, moves slowly."

"Last one down's a landsman." With that, Ham stepped over the edge. The rest followed suit, taking about six seconds to make the drop to the deck. When they landed, they looked about in wonder.

"I think we've found them," said Michelle.

They were standing in another, narrower, corridor, in the biggest room any of them had seen. It seemed to stretch to infinity in both directions, like the corridor above, but it wasn't confined between walls. Along both sides were racks of glasslike cylinders, stacked almost to the ceiling. At regular intervals, narrow lanes ran at right angles from the main corridor into rows of racks as far as the eye could see.

The cylinders lay on their sides, about one and one-half meters long and two-thirds meter in diameter. One end sprouted a system of wires and tubes, the other was flat and featureless. Inside, beings floated in a clear liquid.

The creatures were flattish and circular, slightly domed on the upper surface, the lower surface was flat and covered with tiny-mushroom-shaped protrusions, possibly the creatures' feet. Around the circumference of the body were dozens of appendages ranging from threadlike cilia to tentacles as thick as a man's thumb and sixty centimeters long. The bigger tentacles were flat on the lower side and ridged on the top, apparently for gripping power. The skin was smooth and peach-colored. The small nodules between certain tentacles might have been eyes or sensory organs of some other kind.

"Anybody see a mouth?"

"There's a small slit between two of the smaller tentacles on this one, Ham," Nancy said. "Could be a mouth."

"Will some of you kindly hold still long enough for me to get a look at one of those things?" the skipper asked. "Nancy, do a slow scan and show me every part of one. Ham, will those cylinders lift free?"

"I think so."

"Good. Then bring a couple back with you. They shouldn't be too heavy to carry in that gravity. Do you think those are the creatures that built the ship?"

"The size is in keeping with the spiral ramp," Nancy said.

"They look even softer than you people!" K'Stin noted. "Still, if they *did* build this ship, then they were a great and powerful race, and not to be despised."

"Could be livestock," Torwald said. "Or maybe embryos."

"Useless to speculate," said Ham. "Kelly, you and Lafayette each take an end of this thing and hoist it off the rack. Be sure to take care of the little box those wires go into."

The two did as they were instructed, lifting one of the cylinders free and carrying it to the bottom of the spiral ramp. They then attached lines around it, climbed to the main corridor deck, and hoisted the thing up, an easy task in the weak gravity field. Carrying the cylinder back to the ship was a tedious task, and Kelly fretted because he was missing the further exploration of the alien vessel. Soon after they had the cylinder stowed, under the skipper's careful direction, Finn and Achmed showed up with a second, which was similarly disposed of.

The exploration of the alien vessel proceeded for the next few days, the *Angel*'s crew making as complete a visual record as they could manage, and picking up a few souvenirs here and there. They were compelled, for lack of space, to confine their gathering to small items. Sphere found nothing to his interest in the ship's memory banks, but informed them that the builders of the ship had been in search of a new home planet, in anticipation of the blowup of their own sun. The derelict had been one of thousands of identical vessels.

The second ship was different.

"What is this thing, Skipper, a flying palace?" Torwald asked as he scanned the towering spires around him.

"That's what we're here to find out, Tor."

They were standing in the center of what appeared to be a plaza, surrounded by towers, domes, tetrahedra, and structures in the shape of just about every possible configuration of solid geometry. A gravity field was still working at full efficiency, and they were standing comfortably at something near Earth-normal. They faced the center of the platter-shaped craft, where a cluster of structures towered kilometers upward. Beyond the central cluster, the crew could make out the bulk of the immigrant ship, which had impaled the platter near the far edge.

"They must have maintained a field that kept in their atmosphere," said Bert.

"It didn't keep that ship out, though," the skipper observed. "I'd say that central complex is the best place to start looking. Let's go." They began the long walk to the center of the platter, their boots making prints in the thin layer of dust that the ship's gravity had attracted over thousands of years. They passed what appeared to be parks or gardens, their plantings long since turned to dust. All longed to examine the buildings they were passing, but the huge structures at the center promised better pickings.

From time to time, they came upon sculptures, but most seemed abstract and probably conveyed no idea of what the inhabitants of the ship had looked like. At regular intervals, they passed large, skeletal structures that looked as if they had once supported something, but all were empty. A good deal was speculated about the function of these objects, until Torwald hit upon the likely explanation. "I'll bet those things are lifeboat racks. The crew and passengers must have had time to evacuate before the other ship struck. That's why they're all empty."

The skipper agreed. "You're probably right. If so, they must have left plenty behind. You don't take much except necessities on a lifeboat—what have we here?" Before them another statue occupied a low pedestal; this sculpture was not abstract, but a realistic representation of a being remarkably human in appearance, though the legs and arms were very long and slender and its torso much too thin in the eyes of humans. The hands each bore six long, tapered fingers, and the fingers had at least four joints each. The head was quite human, with rather rectangular eyes. The nose consisted of two vertical slits, and the mouth was lipless and very wide. The alien seemed to be smiling. There was some graceful lettering on the pedestal.

"So that's what they looked like," said Torwald. "At least it's more reassuring than those giant oysters on the other ship."

After several minutes of excited discussion and frenetic recording, the crew hurried onward to the platter's center.

The first building of the central cluster was a few paces beyond the statue. The main doorway was sealed by an airlock, which proved easy to decipher and operate. Once again, they stood inside an alien air-lock as it filled with air.

"Analysis?" said the skipper.

"You can breathe it!" Michelle said. "Pressure's a little lower than we're used to, but everything we need is in it, and nothing that'll do us any harm."

"All right, everybody, unhelm," said the skipper, "but be ready to rehelm at a second's notice."

They took off their helmets and felt their ears pop in the lighter air pressure. The air seemed quite fresh and carried no odor. They hardly had a chance to comment on their good luck when the door before them slid open noiselessly.

Once again, they marveled. The first ship had been so spare and functional that much of its strangeness was cushioned by simplicity. This craft was completely different. The first room was entirely upholstered in a sheer fabric dusted with stylized embroidered stars and flowers. Vases and pitchers, cushions, and odd spindly furniture vied in ornateness with sculpture and hanging mobiles. Everything was so highly embellished that it was difficult to tell the functional from the decorative, if, indeed, the owners had even made such a distinction. Some slight disarray was apparent, but not the utter devastation they had been expecting.

"They had something a lot more powerful than any grav field," the skipper commented. "The impact of the spindle plowing into this should have destroyed the whole interior."

The next room was covered with murals depicting slender humanoids engaged in various activities, mostly incomprehensible. Everywhere were the sculptures, of metal, of crystal, of stone, some mobile and some stationary, some projecting strange lights and colors, some singing to themselves in an unfamiliar musical scale. In another cabin they located large bowls and tiers of shell-like basins, which began to fill with colored liquids as they crossed the threshold.

Lights played through the liquid and struck reflections from glittery hanging sculptures. Sergei used his instruments to make a chemical analysis of one of the liquids.

"It's mostly water," he reported, "but heavily tinged with acids, sugars, and carbohydrates. At a guess, I'd say these fountains are running wine."

"Do you realize what we have here?" Torwald exclaimed. "This is a spacer's dream, a hedonist's paradise, floating adrift in space. It's cloud-cuckoo land. We used to talk about discovering something like this on long watches in the Navy."

"Did the aliens live like this all the time, I wonder, or was this a luxury liner?" Finn mused.

They jerked around in surprise when apertures opened in the wall behind them and small wheeled machines rolled out. The machines ignored them and rolled to the fountains. Some extruded trays bearing crystal goblets and began filling them with a siphon.

"They were an indolent bunch." Michelle stared about her, mouth agape. "They couldn't even be bothered with filling their own glasses."

"They built to last, though," the skipper said. "Come on, let's look for the control center. That's where the records and memory banks will be." She led the way out, taking a bearing on her directional indicator. They managed to cross three rooms before coming to an abrupt halt. The fourth was a banquet hall, with rows of low tables flanked by cushions. The tables were set, with small robots scurrying about, bringing out new dishes, pouring flagons of beverages. They all sniffed.

"Smells good," Kelly said tentatively. The crew had been eating freezedrys for a long time now.

"Hold it!" the skipper yelled. "Nobody touches that stuff until Michelle makes an analysis. Just because they breathe the same mixture we do doesn't mean their food won't poison us."

"It won't poison us," K'Stin noted caustically.

"You two could probably eat the sculpture. Go ahead." The Vivers sat and started shoveling in the fare on the table. Vivers were conditioned to be abstemious with food when it was in short supply, but they could consume incredible amounts when it was unlimited, storing the excess as fat within their thoracic and abdominal cavities.

"The metals and plastics I can understand," Finn mused, "but, how can those food items have lasted this long? From the accumulation of space dust outside, I'd guess this ship has been abandoned for millennia."

"They must be synthesized from chemical tanks, Finn," said Nancy. "We've been trying to solve that problem for years. Just keep supplies of the right molecules on hand, feed the proper formula into the control computer, and instant lobster Newburg."

"If we could get the secret of that and take it back home," said the skipper, "it would be worth millions of times the value of all that diamond crystal in the hold."

"These dishes are all right, except for that green jelly," Michelle said. She proceeded to the next setting. "The jelly won't kill you, but it will act as a violent laxative."

"While we're waiting for the verdict on the rest," the skipper said, "we might as well get a little exploring done. Torwald, you and Kelly look in that room there." She pointed to her right. "Finn and Nancy, look into that one." She pointed left. "Achmed, you and Bert take those stairs and check out the room up there. Bring back anything intriguing and portable. Sergei, help Michelle with her chemical analyses."

The room Kelly and Torwald explored seemed empty, its floor bearing only some cushions like those around the banquet tables. The walls were free of murals, and there were none of the by now inevitable sculptures.

"Now, what could—" Torwald's question was cut off abruptly when, without warning, a figure appeared before them. The alien was about seven feet high, clad in a close-fitting garment of silvery blue. Its skin was pale yellow, and its eyes were translucent green, without white, iris, or pupil. It made a gesture resembling a bow, its mouth moving in speech, but making no sound. Kelly and Torwald reached for their pistols, then stopped as the figure made no threatening move.

"It isn't possible, Tor! The ship and furnishings, yes. The food, maybe, but not a living alien!"

"Not living, I don't think," Torwald commented tersely. He reached out and placed his fingers against the being's chest. They encountered no resistance, just disappeared into the chest. The figure continued its pantomime of speech without taking notice. "It's some kind of holographic projection. We must have activated it when we entered the room." The figure disappeared and the lights went out.

Suddenly, the walls came to life with light and color. Streaks and balls and particles of multicolored light darted through the air, seeming to pass through their bodies. Alien music wafted through the chamber, and they sat down to enjoy the show. Some of the flying bits of light merged and coalesced into the likenesses of weird creatures. The creatures danced and darted to the alien music, then burst into thousands of particles once more. Enthralled, Kelly lost track of time, until he felt a tap on the back of his head. It was Torwald, beckoning him to leave. Reluctantly, he did so.

Back in the banqueting hall, they found the others sitting on the cushions.

"We were about to come looking for you."

"You missed the best show in town, Skipper. Kelly and I just found a theater of some kind, complete with a hologram alien emcee."

"We're about to start in on this, Tor. Michelle's

cleared all the stuff on this table. The inedible stuff is over there." The skipper gestured at a stack of dishes on another table.

Torwald and Kelly seated themselves and looked at their companions, waiting for somebody else to take the first bite. The others were doing the same.

"Oh, come on, it's safe," the skipper said. "Kelly, you first."

With some trepidation, Kelly picked up an object resembling an egg roll and bit into it. It tasted like a meat and vegetable combination, rather spicy. He swallowed and waited for aftereffects. Nothing happened.

"Pretty good," Kelly announced. The rest dug in.

"This sauce tastes like glue," Nancy said with a sour look.

"The fruit salad's not bad," pronounced Torwald. They picked about at various dishes and found some delicious, some objectionable, a few revolting. Few of the flavors were comparable to anything they had tasted on Earth or on any of the inhabited planets. The strangeness of the situation was apparent to them all: they were sitting down to a feast laid out for aliens who had departed millennia before.

When they could hold no more, they resumed the search for the control center, passing through more rooms of artistic wonder until they came to a huge room that looked to be part control room, part library. At its center was a cluster of instrument panels with screens and gauges. The walls were covered with shelves of books, scrolls, and other objects that might have been data storage devices. The books were written in a multitude of scripts, some using embossed marks like braille rather than writing.

"We might have known that people as aesthetic as these would be book collectors, too. Now, what's that?" The skipper's question was about yet another strange creature which appeared to be walking toward them. If it resembled anything in their experience, it was a crab—its shell was about a meter across, and between its upper and lower halves, various limbs protruded, some tipped with lobsterlike nippers, some with graspers like those of a praying mantis. Tiny eyes on stems seemed to regard them without fear or threat.

"I wonder how they made these projections so realistic?" Kelly mused, leaning over to pass his fingers through the image as Torwald had done with the one in the theater. To his alarm, his fingers rapped on solid shell, whereupon the others scrambled backward and reached for their weapons. They stood there indecisively, their guns trained on the thing, when they were shaken by the sound of hooting laughter. It was Ham, his voice coming over the ship-to-suit.

"All right, Ham, what's so funny?"

"If you people aren't a sight, Gertie!" He was still gurgling with laughter. "Eleven people, including two big Vivers, standing around and pointing guns at an overgrown crab! If you could see your faces!" He trailed off into another laughing fit.

"The humor of the situation is not apparent," the skipper growled. "We'll discuss that later." Despite her words, there was a general relaxing of tensions, and most of the standard humans holstered their weapons. The Vivers kept theirs trained steadily upon the crustacean.

"It doesn't seem threatening," said Michelle, tentatively.

This one is intelligent. More so than you. It means no harm to you. Set me on one of those instrument consoles.

That was the first communication from Sphere since they had boarded the second ship. Sphere had been increasingly uncommunicative of late. They wanted to know more about the strange creature, but Sphere seemed uninterested in enlightening them further.

When Achmed and the skipper returned to the ship to relieve Ham and Lafayette, the crab-thing followed them. The rest looked through the books in the library *cum* control room. They had ceased trying to figure out the peculiar phenomena they were encountering.

Ham and Lafayette arrived some hours later, wearing expressions of contentment.

"Hey, thanks for screening that food for us," Lafayette said. "Ham and I stuck to the stuff you passed as the best eating."

"Yeah. It takes a lot of the anxiety out of a meal when you've had someone else taste it first." The rest regarded them without favor.

"You're just getting back at us for being the first on this ship while you two stayed on the *Angel*," said Michelle.

"What happened to the crab, Ham?" Finn asked.

"You know, that little critter followed the skipper back to the ship. Walked right across the open spaces without any life-support apparatus. Either it can hold its breath for a long time, or it can breathe vacuum."

"The little being rises in my estimation, thus placing it somewhat above you weak things. It is of a seemly adaptability." K'Stin was unable to mask the admiration that had crept into his voice.

"What's the crab doing now, Ham?" Torwald asked.

"When I left, it was playing with the computer. The skipper put all the crucial functions on manual override, for whatever that's worth with Sphere on board, but the little crab didn't seem interested in any mechanical capabilities. It looked over a single read-out and then punched out a code for language instruction. I think it'll be able to understand us pretty soon. It didn't bother with human-speed learning. It took the information at computer-to-computer data transfer rates."

"The little being has excellent mechanical-mathematical aptitude as well as extreme capabilities of passive survival. If only it were aggressive and pugnacious, it would be a most admirable creature."

"It's possible that not everybody finds those qualities as indispensible as you do, K'Stin." Indignation marred Nancy's normally expressionless face.

"Possibly not, weak creature. Just as well. That gives us an edge."

We will return to the ship. Nothing remains in these instruments that is of use to me. We must go farther toward the Center.

"But, we've just begun to make records of this ship!" Ham protested.

That is of no concern to me. I need other information.

They could not fight the thing's will, so they reluctantly returned to the ship, carrying as many books as they could handle and several of the smaller sculptures. Once aboard the *Angel,* they found the crablike thing squatting on a seat in the mess. It extruded a few eyes to regard them and wiggled some antennae toward them for some purpose.

They were joined by the skipper, who had been on the bridge. "Sphere's taken us into hyper again. Too bad. I could've spent the rest of my life on those ships. Oh, well—"

"If there is something you wish to know about that craft or the people who built it, you need only ask." The crab had spoken.

"That was quick," the skipper yelped.

"I have an aptitude for languages."

"Who are you, and what were you doing aboard that derelict?" asked Ham.

"My name would be difficult to translate into your tongue, but it means something like 'He Sings the Praises of Great Beings and Their Deeds in Elegant Verse Forms.' That is a somewhat abbreviated version, of course, lacking the rhythm and resonance of the original."

"It'll do," said the skipper.

"As for why I was aboard that ship, I was collecting material."

"Material for what?"

"For my poems."

"How did you get there?"

"I was visiting a world of a nearby system when this wreckage was detected by instruments. I requested passage to the vessels so that I could examine them. That was some time ago, and they have not returned for me. I suppose they have forgotten me, or perhaps a war has intervened." The voice seemed to emanate from within the shell.

"How long ago was that?" the skipper asked.

"By your time, six or seven hundred years."

"What's that amount to by your time?"

"A rather brief span. I spent it quite enjoyably, going over the vast literature contained in that ship. The Hubri were a great race, perhaps the most aesthetic people who ever lived. As patrons of the arts, they were beyond compare. They cruised the center systems for many centuries, then disappeared perhaps a thousand years ago, searching for new artistic experiences. Naturally, I jumped at the chance to study aboard one of their splendid pleasure craft."

"Jumped too soon, it seems," the skipper commented.

"All turned out well." The crab seemed to shrug its shell.

"Well," said Torwald, "it seems that you're going to be traveling with us for a while. That being the case, we'd better give you a name that's more convenient to us. Any suggestions?"

"An early Terran poet of note was one named Homer. In a crude way, his verses were of great power, although *Beowulf* had far more moral force than his works. You may call me Homer, if you like."

"Homer it is, then," Ham said. Then he introduced Michelle, who'd been tugging at the left sleeve of his coverall.

"I'm in charge of diet and health. First of all, what do you eat?"

"Anything composed primarily of organic molecules; all animal or vegetable matter or by-products. Even petroleum will do—"

Unable to restrain himself, K'Stin suddenly interrupted the crab. "You were able to survive in the vacuum without breathing apparatus. How did you do that?"

"Oh, my race can last for lengthy periods without breathing. When necessary, by keeping perfectly still we can last for many centuries without drawing a breath. This becomes tedious, of course. Also, I can breathe chlorine, methane, helium, and a number of other gases besides oxygen."

K'Stin nodded. Torwald thought he detected approval in the Viver's manner.

"Michelle, you needn't worry about my health. I don't suffer from illness, and all injuries are repaired within a few days without treatment or medication."

"Little creature, it is extremely unlikely that any single planet would have an atmosphere suitable for evolving creatures able to breathe such a profusion of gases. You did not evolve, did you? You were designed, like us Vivers."

"But, of course. Originally, my race were soft-bodied mollusks, rather like the creatures you found on the spindle ship. We found that something more durable would be better suited for exploring diverse worlds. You see before you one of the results. Many other, more specialized forms were developed, but we traveling poets and scholars prefer this form."

"It seems well-suited to survival," K'Stin admitted grudgingly, "but not as good for fighting as ours."

"Probably so, but then, belligerent species tend to have brief histories. The records of my race go back two million years." The Viver lapsed into sulky silence, much to the amusement of the others.

What do you know of the Core Star?

They started slightly. They had almost forgotten Sphere.

"Who is addressing me?" asked Homer.

"That ball in the middle of the table." The skipper replied, pointing at Sphere. "It's controlling things on the *Angel* these days. It's taken us on a quest for the Core Star, which it claims resides in the center of the galaxy."

"I am quite familiar with the phenomenon. What, specifically, did you wish to know about it? I must warn you, I am not a physicist."

I want to know about a nonastronomical phenomenon that I believe might be residing near the Core Star.

"Oh," said Homer, "do you refer to the Guardian?"

The humans looked at one another. Yet another mystery had been introduced.

"The Guardian?" Ham's voice was wary.

That is the phenomenon to which I refer.

"I cannot tell you much about it, since so little is known. Seemingly without shape or form, it resides in the great empty zone between the last conventional stars and the Core Star. It has been there since intelligent life first developed space travel in the Center area, and it will not let anything approach closer than a hundred light-years to the Core Star. Every scientific probe and military expedition has been destroyed or repulsed. That is the body of knowledge concerning the creature. Theories, of course, are rife concerning its nature and origin. Some hold that it is intelligent, others that it is a forcefield phenomenon, others that it is a device invented by a very early race, possibly one from another galaxy. One guess is as good as another, in the absence of data."

That is what I wished to know.

Sphere said no more that day.

Six

A few days later, the *Space Angel* once again emerged from hyper in a strange system. The crew had spent the intervening time getting acquainted with Homer. They found him to be a friendly little creature and a repository of information about the center stars, among which he had been traveling for many thousands of years, collecting the poetry of hundreds of races. His own specialty was heroic verse. Even the Vivers were forced to admire him, if only for his extreme longevity.

Homer was also a gifted teacher, and Kelly spent many hours with him, absorbing the history and literature that the State schools had not bothered to teach. From the ship's computers, Homer had absorbed the full body of human literature and history. If Kelly survived, he would be a tolerably well-educated man by the end of the voyage.

They were in the midst of a lesson when the ship's klaxon sounded an alarm. Kelly dashed to his battle station, the assistant's chair in the six-beam cutter installation, which was now located in the navigator's bubble.

"What's happened, Torwald?" he demanded, dropping into the deep padded chair and strapping himself in.

"We're under attack," Torwald was calmly testing his controls.

"We came out of hyper a few minutes ago," Ham shouted from his station at the controls of the depolarizer he and Nancy crewed. "There was a planet nearby, a gas giant the size of Jupiter. We were looking for a more congenial place when the shooting started. A battle station is orbiting the gas giant, but it must've been on the far side when we came out of hyper. Soon as it cleared the horizon, though, it let us have both barrels. Force weapons of some kind. Sphere's deflecting most of it, but we're taking some damage."

"Why doesn't Sphere jump us into hyper out of here?" Kelly asked, staring through the blister overhead as his hands performed the adjustments Torwald had drilled into him. Space around the ship was ashimmer with brilliant colors.

"We think Sphere's preoccupied with neutralizing that thing's attacks."

Finn chimed in from below, "According to my instruments, Sphere's moving us away from the battle station. I hope we're out of range soon."

Suddenly, Kelly's eyes were dazzled by an especially brilliant display of pyrotechnics and the ship rocked. The damage alarm shrieked through the ship, and the group in the bubble scrambled into their life-support suits.

"What's the damage?" demanded Ham, securing his helmet.

"The hull's been ruptured between hold hatches two and three. Everything abaft Hydroponic's been sealed off," the skipper's voice was as calm as if she were reading a bill of lading.

"Anybody back there?" Torwald asked.

"No. Everyone's forward."

Gradually, the colors surrounding them faded. There were no more shocks.

"We seem to be out of range." The skipper sounded relieved. "Achmed, take Lafayette and Kelly aft and make a damage assessment. Everybody else stand to battle stations until I give further orders."

Kelly unstrapped himself and made his way down to the lower companionway, then back past Hydroponics to the big bulkhead that separated the forward part of the ship from the hold. There he met Achmed and Lafayette, standing at the emergency lock.

"We'll have to go through one at a time," the Muslim stated. "I'll go first, then Lafayette, then you, Kelly. Beyond that door we're in vacuum until we can effect repairs. Keep that in mind." Achmed opened the lock hatch and stepped inside. The hatch closed and they heard a hissing as the air was expelled from the interior. Next Lafayette went in, then it was Kelly's turn.

As the hatch opening on the hold cycled open, Kelly held his breath. He expected utter devastation: the ship's hull ripped open, the cargo of crystal shattered, the catwalk dangling precariously from its supports or gone altogether. He saw nothing of the sort. Everything seemed normal. That in itself was a sobering concept; it brought home to him what a fragile environment the ship provided, and that even a seemingly trivial bit of damage could turn what had become a secure home to him into a coffin floating forever in the spaces between the stars.

He shook off the mood and entered, moving cautiously to where Achmed and Lafayette stood at the aft end of the catwalk. They were staring at something overhead. When Kelly joined them, he could see what held their attention. Near the aft bulkhead, the skin of the ship showed a narrow rent, no more than ten centimeters wide and about two meters long, as if a giant razor had sliced neatly into the ship and then passed on. The end of the slice disappeared beyond the bulkhead separating the hold from the installations in the tail of the ship.

"That rent goes into the AC dock, Kelly. You go into the dock and check out the damage there while Lafayette and I rig a patch here."

Kelly edged past the bulkhead and took the ladder to the upper deck, where he pushed the dock hatch open and stepped inside. From the bulkhead, the slit in the skin continued for another three meters and then tapered to nothing. The thick-clustered stars shone through it as a band of malevolent beauty. Whatever had cut the skin had also hit the AC. The tail of the craft showed deep slices through the rear stabilizing vanes and propulsion cones.

"Achmed, the AC's damaged, and there's more skin rupture in here than in the hold." His voice sounded unfamiliar to him in the helmet.

"*Damn.* Does the hole go back as far as the aft bulkhead?"

"No, it ends about a third of the way there."

"Well, that's something. I think we can rig a patch. It'll last for a while, but we'll have to put down on a planet for proper repairs before we travel much farther. How bad is the damage to the AC?"

"I'm no expert, but it looks bad. Some plates cut through completely, and there's damage to the drive." That could be serious. If they were to do any planetside work, the atmosphere craft would be essential.

For the next few hours, Kelly was kept busy running for materials while Achmed, Torwald, and K'Stin rigged a patch. Kelly and Lafayette had to wrestle sheets of metal from the supply room, cut them into pieces small enough to pass through the emergency lock, then carry them through the hold, where they were welded into place.

During the repair work, the skipper cruised the system, looking for a planet suitable to land on for more thorough repairs. Nearer the system's sun, she spotted a likely prospect. Several days were required to reach the planet, and the crew became increasingly nervous as they neared it. The gas giant had been protected by a battle station; this place might be, too.

Their fears proved groundless. The planet loomed overhead, as seen through the dome of the navigation bubble. Mostly ocean, but two sizable continents visible, and a number of large islands. Most of the landmass was obscured by clouds, but what could be seen was bright green.

"Where shall we land, Gertie?" Ham asked. "That peninsula on the southeast coast of the northern continent looks like a good spot."

"There's a tropical storm heading that way. Let's try that big island just south of the equator. Instrument readings show no signs of advanced, technological civilization down there, but let's not take chances. If there is such a culture, an island is the last place it will be. We need a few days without disturbance to carry out repairs, and we can't afford a fight with anybody who can match our firepower."

Finn descended to his navigation room and returned a few minutes later. "I've located a good-sized clearing in the uplands, well away from the ocean."

"That'll do," the skipper said. "We'll set down there, and work on repairs. Nobody leaves the landing area without permission. All right, everybody, back to your cabins and prepare to land. When we're down, I'll call off work parties. We've got some crucial repairs to make and I don't want to waste any time."

They filed out. Kelly, for one, was disappointed that they wouldn't be doing any exploring. He suspected that he wasn't alone.

Kelly and Nancy stood at the top of the ramp.

Ham, Achmed, and Bert were working the first shift repairing the *Angel*'s hull. The AC would be tended to later, and without it, the skipper had ruled out any exploring.

"What a waste!" Kelly observed bitterly. "A whole new world, untouched by humans, and we can't so much as set foot on it. Doesn't it make you mad?" He was hoping to elicit some kind of personal revelation from Nancy. Since the day she had revealed something of her childhood, she had withdrawn once more into her untouchable shell when she was alone with him.

"I've seen lots of new worlds, Kelly, some of them never explored before. You get used to it. And the skipper's right. It just looks like an Earth jungle. It could be something completely different. That stuff that looks like grass could be carnivorous, for instance. Flowers could spray poison gas in your face. Animals could dig camouflaged pits for you to step in. I've seen such things on colonized worlds. This place is an unknown quantity."

"We could send the Vivers out to look around. They're not afraid of anything."

"They wouldn't risk themselves without a pressing reason. Besides, the skipper can't order them out just to satisfy our curiosity. And, they're afraid of everything until it's proven harmless; then they keep an eye on it, just in case."

"Those two worry about their survival so much, I wonder why they don't die of anxiety." Kelly laughed at his own joke. It struck him that it had been a long time since he'd last laughed.

"What's the joke?" came a voice behind them. Lafayette stepped out onto the gangway platform. He was looking surly this morning. The last few weeks, even Kelly had noticed that the long voyage and the strain of uncertainty were telling on Lafayette.

"Kelly made an observation concerning the Vivers," Nancy answered blandly. Kelly looked at her.

Did he detect a glint of complicity in her eye? He decided that he didn't. She always looked like that.

"A lot of good those two lobsters have done us so far," Lafayette commented. "Teddy's been as much help, and even Homer at least breaks up the monotony."

"I'm going back to the comm room," Nancy announced, obviously not wishing to be around Lafayette in this mood. He didn't seem to notice when she left.

"Hey, Kelly, what do you say we go have a look around? This ship's about to drive me into a permanent Whoopee Drive dream."

"I don't know," said Kelly, doubtfully. "The skipper said—"

"Who cares what she said! She's not human, anyway. What's she going to do, kick us off the ship? Chances are, we'll never get back from this crazy trip whatever we do."

"Well, suit yourself, but I'm staying here," said Kelly, although he really wanted to go.

"Stay here, then!" Lafayette yelled. He stalked down the ramp and onto the ground, not even pausing to make a speech appropriate to being the first human to set foot on a new world. He crossed the clearing and disappeared into the jungle. Kelly waited for him to return, and after an hour had passed, he began to grow alarmed. When he could wait no longer, he headed for the bridge, where the skipper was going over some drawings with Ham, Torwald, and Michelle. She looked up as he entered, frowned when she caught his worried expression.

"What's the matter?" she asked.

"Lafayette's left the ship," he said.

"What?" She jumped out of her chair, ran to Kelly and grabbed him by the shoulders. "When?"

"A little over an hour ago. He—"

"Over an hour ago?" Her wrath mounted by the second. "Why did you wait so long to tell me, you

117

landsman?" The deadly insult warned Kelly that he was in deep trouble. With trepidation, he explained what had happened.

"Why didn't you stop him?"

"It was his neck, wasn't it? He knew your orders."

"You should've stopped him."

"How, Skipper?"

"You could've punched him out," said Torwald. "You've done that before."

"We're wasting time," said the skipper. "Torwald, fetch the gear you'll need for a ground expedition. Send the Vivers out first to scout for his trail. Send Homer, too. He can see and sense things we can't. Take everybody who isn't needed to repair the AC. When that's fixed, it'll be a lot easier looking. Michelle, I hate to send you along, but he's liable to need immediate medical care when he's found. *If* he's found. Get going. *You* stay here," she said, pointing at Kelly. When the others had gone, she thrust her face within an inch of Kelly's. She had to stretch to do it. He had been growing.

"Listen, you. When you serve in a ship, you think of the ship first, last, and always. Your temper and feelings don't count. That boy has been at the breaking point for weeks, and it was your job to look out for him, whatever differences you two have had in the past. You've let a shipmate down, you've forced the rest of the crew to endanger their lives, and you've endangered the ship. Those are three unforgivable sins. Now, against my better judgment, I'm going to give you a chance to redeem yourself. You're going out with that party. If Lafayette doesn't come back with them, I don't want to see you back, either." She turned and strode through the hatch, leaving Kelly pale and shaken, alone on the bridge.

The Vivers and Homer returned from the jungle within an hour.

"His trail was clear for nearly a kilometer," K'Stin

reported, "then it disappeared. The remains of a snare were found where his tracks ended. No sign of blood, no tracks leading away."

"It is my opinion," said Homer, "that the locals have spirited him away through the trees, and the Vivers and I are not arboreal."

"See anything else?" the skipper asked.

"Heavy jungle," said K'Stin, "many animals, large and small. Some predators, nothing to trouble a Viver, but you soft ones will have to be careful. Also found some big stone buildings about five kilometers from here, but there was a lot of jungle growth on them, so they are probably uninhabited."

"All right, then," the skipper said. "First task: check out those buildings. Look for signs of life—intelligent life. Keep in regular contact with the ship and take no unnecessary chances. Get going."

The party was equipped for a long hike through difficult terrain, without arm- and leg-armor, just body armor and puncture-proof coveralls. Everyone wore belted laser handguns and machetes; Ham and Torwald carried forcebeam rifles in addition. The Vivers were, as usual, walking arsenals. They crossed the clearing and within moments the jungle had swallowed them up.

In spite of their serious mission, the Earthmen stared with fascination at their exotic surroundings: one tree with a spirally fluted trunk sprouting a crown of feathery blue leaves fifty meters from the ground, another bristling with long spikes, vines that crept along the ground, and others looping from one treetop to another; and everywhere there were flowers. Some were so tiny that clusters of hundreds of blooms made a mass no bigger than a fingertip, others so large that a single petal measured two paces across.

They walked into wave after wave of odor, from the most delicate of perfumes to the rankest stenches. Every plant in the jungle seemed to call attention to itself, with outlandish form, outrageous color, inescapable aroma, or a combination of all three. Animals were apparent in equal profusion and variety. Some were small, many-legged insect equivalents; scaly creatures, some legless, that appeared to be reptiles; furry beasts of all sizes that might have been mammals. There were no birds or anything with feathers, but many species of the other three types flew. The air was alive with flying insects, and big creatures with translucent wings chased the bugs. At one point a little thing, vaguely reptiloid, with wings landed on Kelly's shoulder and studied his face through jewellike, golden eyes.

To Kelly's relief, the little dragon flapped silently away after a few moments of careful contemplation.

The relatively open forest near the clearing soon gave way to dense undergrowth and the Vivers, in the lead as usual, began plying their sword-length machetes. Their arms rose and fell mechanically, shearing through tough, woody vines as easily as if they were daisy stalks. A kilometer of such growth would have taken standard humans all day to cut through. The Vivers covered that distance in a little less than an hour.

The stifling humidity soon had the standard humans' bodies streaming with sweat, despite the sophisticated air-circulation systems implanted in their coveralls. Sweat squished in their boots and ran from their sleeves into their gloves. Even the light body armor began to chafe and their packs to weigh heavily. The Vivers, of course, seemed perfectly comfortable, as did Homer, who burbled away, composing complex verses in some language or other. The standard humans were relieved when K'Stin called a halt.

The party had halted along the edge of a slowly moving stream about twenty meters across. The water was murky and looked ominous. Occasionally, the surface was marked with a chain of V's as something large and swift swam just below the surface. B'Shant plucked a large blossom and tossed it into the water. Immediately, the surface was disturbed as something shot toward the flower. The searchers received the impression of a scaly snout amid a spray of water—the blossom was gone. A few seconds later, it reemerged as ragged fragments, spat out in disappointment by the hungry reptiloid.

"I, for one, don't care to dispute right of passage with those things," Finn admitted.

"There is no problem," K'Stin said. "Get ready to cross." Without waiting for a reply, he barked an order to B'Shant. The other Viver picked three more of the big flowers and tossed them into the water about twenty meters downstream. Three heads appeared almost simultaneously to snatch the blooms. This time, though, the Vivers shot them as soon as their heads appeared above the surface. The beams, set for cutting action, sliced deep, filling the water with dark-blue blood. As the dead creatures thrashed in nervous reaction, dozens of wakes converged upon them. In seconds, the water was churned into spray as carnivores battled one another for possession of this bounty.

"Cross now!" K'Stin commanded. Nervously, the others obeyed, holding weapons high, while the Vivers remained on the bank, scanning the water, beam rifles ready. As soon as the others were across, B'Shant crossed, then K'Stin as B'Shant watched from the opposite bank. Halfway across, K'Stin was yanked abruptly from view. A few seconds later he reappeared, wrapped in the coils of some long serpent, one that seemed to be equipped with tentacles. K'Stin located the thing's head and seized it, yanking it upward over his own. As soon as the ugly head was clear of K'Stin's body, B'Shant put a needlebeam neatly through its eye. Immediately, the beast dropped loose and K'Stin waded ashore without further ado.

"Homer, you didn't mention these creatures before. Were they here on your last visit, along with the fragrances and flowers?"

"Possibly so, Ham, but the inhabitants may no longer be keeping them in check. Or, perhaps, this is an area kept deliberately wild. In any case, none of these creatures is dangerous to me, so they may have made no impression. It was long ago and my memory falters at such a span."

"If it was millennia ago, your memory may be excused for slipping a little," Torwald noted.

The Vivers resumed their mechanical trail-clearing and the rest followed, sweating and puffing. None of them had had so much planetside activity in months; everyone was out of shape. Another hour passed and they were within sight of the buildings, which the Vivers had spotted earlier. First, the party could make out the tops of the structures through gaps between the trees, then lower levels appeared. Suddenly, they were free of the trees and gawking with wonder. Before them stood a wall built of gigantic stone blocks, twenty meters high and stretching away on either hand as far as the eye could discern. From behind the wall they could see the mammoth buildings, tall towers and massive, stepped, pyramidal structures, all wildly and grotesquely decorated.

"Primitive-looking, eh, Kelly?"

"That's primitive? What do you think, Torwald? It looks pretty advanced to me."

"All it takes is wealth and manpower to build like that, kid. Building on this scale has been done by people not yet out of the Stone Age. Let's save our judgment for later, though. How're we going to get over that wall?"

"We will climb to the top," said K'Stin. "Then we will lower ropes for you." Suiting actions to words, the Vivers began climbing straight up the wall, their claws finding holds in crevices that were barely visible to those on the ground. Homer simply walked up the wall as easily as if it had been a horizontal surface. From the top, the Vivers dropped their ropes.

"Don't try to climb, we will pull you up," said K'Stin. Ham and Torwald were first to grasp the ropes at the knotted handholds. Seemingly without effort, the Vivers hauled the two heavy men to the top. The first thing the two realized when they had reached the top was that the "wall" was actually a platform, apparently of solid masonry. The buildings they had seen were constructed atop this cyclopean terrace.

The stone of the terrace was worn smooth from the passage of centuries, greenish-gray streaked with yellow. The buildings were a riot of noisy color, as garish as the jungle had been, faced with slabs of alabaster, speckled porphyries, colorful marbles in all hues. Every surface was carved with figures, interlaced designs, or abstract patterns. All the edifices were heavily garlanded by jungle growth. Over the centuries, seeds blown by winds or carried by flying creatures had found nooks and crevices where soil had collected, and there they took root. Their roots had widened the cracks, their rotting remains had contributed more humus, and larger plants had replaced them, until, now, full-sized trees were growing on many of the structures, their huge, gnarled roots separating giant blocks as if they had been children's toys.

"Sergei," Ham asked when the entire party stood atop the platform, "what do you make of this stone?"

"The platform's made of a fairly soft limestone," the geologist said. "It wouldn't be difficult to cut and polish. I'll have to get a closer look at the colored stuff facing the structures."

"Let's try that one, then." Ham pointed to the tallest of the pyramidal edifices, the upper part of which was fairly free of growth. "From that high up we might get some idea where Lafayette's been taken." They set out for the building at a weary but eager pace, their curiosity giving them new energy. At the base, they craned their necks upward. Looming above them were vast stone faces, snarling, four-eyed devil-masks, all of the same type but no two exactly alike, thirty meters from the lowest wattle below their beaky snouts to the top of the finlike crest surmounting their double-domed skulls.

"Now, what might those be, Finn? Gods? Demons? Guardian Spirits? Dead Politicians?"

"Useless to speculate without further data. Anybody see a door?"

They searched around the base and found that the ugly masks continued at intervals of six meters. Below a truly horrifying face, its four eyes made of a translucent green stone, they found a low arched doorway.

"That's a true keystone arch," Nancy observed. "From the style of these structures I'd have expected corbels."

"Whoever these people were," Sergei said, "they had access to offworld materials. The eyes on that mask are made of transparent jadeoid, and that stuff forms only on planets with a high percentage of ammonia in the atmosphere. I can see a few other decorative stones that couldn't have originated on this planet. Of course, the people who built this might have been cannibalizing materials from earlier, spacefaring cultures."

They filed through the arch, the Vivers having to duck low to clear the keystone. Inside, the sudden switch from bright sunlight to interior dimness left the standard humans blinded for a few seconds. They switched on their torches and found that they were in a large square room, its walls covered with what appeared to be writing. They were also inlaid with gold.

"Maybe we should take back a few samples," suggested Torwald. "Not much, just a few dozen kilos apiece. What do you think, Finn? It seems a shame to just let the jungle take over."

"Shame on you, Tor, suggesting such vandalism. Besides, there could be proprietors hereabouts who might object."

"Let's go on," Ham urged. "Plenty of time later to gather souvenirs, after we figure out what we've found." They proceeded through the lower floor, finding more rooms, mostly small, all decorated with gold-inlaid inscriptions. Eventually, they came upon a ramp leading upward. Their explorations continued as they ascended the pyramid, and they encountered more script-carved rooms, the rooms getting larger as they climbed higher. The party found hallways leading to terraces that overlooked the jungle, but nothing to indicate what the building was. There was no sculpture, no sarcophagus, nothing that appeared to be a throne-room.

"Maybe it's the national archives," suggested Torwald. "All this writing could just be rules and regs."

"Or it could be a temple," Nancy offered. "Those walls could be covered with prayers."

"No figures of gods, though," objected Kelly, "unless that's what those masks outside are."

"You won't find god-sculptures in synagogues or mosques, Kelly," said Torwald. "Taboos against picturing a diety are fairly common." They were approaching the last ramp. This one led to a spacious, airy room with large doorways opening onto the top of the pyramid. For the first time since entering the structure, there was no writing on the walls. Instead, the room was perfectly featureless except for a cylindrical dais of stone about a meter high in its center. Capping the dais was a disk of what appeared to be solid gold at least fifteen centimeters thick. The disk was engraved with designs of bewildering complexity. They studied this prodigy for a long time before anyone spoke.

"It looks like a star chart to me," Finn said. "I think that the figures made with straight lines are numbers. It's somewhat stylized, and it's terribly complex, but then, you can see about a thousand times more stars here than you can see from Earth."

"You think they had an astronomical bias?" Ham asked.

"If they built this pyramid and inlaid it with gold for the purpose of setting this disk here, then they surely had some interest in the subject. Perhaps Sphere should inspect this thing."

"I'll relay that suggestion to the skipper," said Ham. "Meanwhile, let's step outside and take a look around while we still have light." The view from the top of the pyramid was breathtaking. The platform upon which the pyramid rested was much larger than they had believed, covering at least ten acres and studded with more of the primitive-sophisticated architecture. Here and there, more of the platforms poked up through the jungle.

"I see smoke coming from one of those complexes," said Kelley, pointing to a smaller platform about three kilometers away.

"There's another," said Michelle, indicating a more distant complex. From both, thin columns of gray smoke were rising into the breezeless air. The sun was beginning to lower, turning a lurid red in the process. The color change turned the jungle and the ruins, exotic to begin with, into as bizarre a sight as any they had ever seen. Ham took out his transmitter and made a brief report of their findings.

"Are you coming back, Ham?"

"It's too late to make it back by nightfall, Gertie. Also, I'd like to get a look at those settlements to see if whoever's making the smoke snatched Lafayette. We'll split up into two parties in the morning and check them out."

"Achmed thinks he can have the AC back in operation by late tomorrow," the skipper informed them. "Send me your position when you're together again and I'll send it out to pick you up. Now, get some rest." Her transmission clicked off.

"As if we needed orders for that," muttered Ham. "All right, people, get your sleeping gear and your rations out. We all stand watch tonight; Sergei, you take first watch with me, Tor, you take second with Kelly, Michelle third, and Finn and Nancy get fourth. You Vivers split it up as you like, I'm not familiar with your sleep patterns. Homer, do you sleep at all?"

"Not after the nesting stage. I think I will go explore the other buildings here. I see quite well in this light."

"We are not as slothful as you soft persons," said K'Stin. "I shall take the first half of the night, and

126

B'Shant shall take the second. We shall watch from the top of this temple or observatory or whatever it is. The roof is too steep for you to stand on, so I suggest that your sentries stay on the terrace. Actually, with such as we standing guard, your feeble senses will be superfluous, anyhow."

"We'll all stand guard, just the same," said Ham.

The party inflated their sleeping-cocoons, then turned their attention to supper. Kelly took a packet of freezedrys from his pack, giving it a squeeze to break the water bladder inside and let the food soak while the packet heated the contents. When ready, the packet popped open and he fished out the enclosed spoon. Numbly, without appetite, he began to eat. The others were doing the same. Too exhausted to speak, they were eating as quickly as possible and rolling into their cocoons, except for Ham and Sergei, who slung their rifles and marched out, followed by K'Stin.

It seemed a mercilessly short time before Kelly was shaken awake. It took several seconds for him to focus on the face above him and recognize it as Torwald's, a few seconds more to remember where he was.

"Time to be up and about," Torwald said cheerfully. Groggily, Kelly rolled out of his cocoon and lurched to his feet. Torwald thrust a rifle into his hands and herded him outside. Kelly began to waken quickly when he stepped onto the terrace. Even with a filtering atmosphere, the night sky was gorgeous beyond belief, the crowded stars shedding a light of about the same intensity as that of a heavily overcast day on Earth. Through the atmospheric filter, the nebulae flickered and twinkled, and some of the variable stars flashed and dimmed like warning lights.

Below, the jungle was making a tremendous racket —squeaks, roars, barks, tweets, rattles, squawks, and many other sounds that defied description. It seemed as if the night life of the jungle relied on sound instead of color to make itself known.

Torwald adjusted Kelly's rifle sling, then added, "It

127

hangs horizontally. The strap goes over your right shoulder and the rifle hangs under your right arm, at about elbow level. You only sling it behind you when you're marching." He looked up. "How's the night, K'Stin?"

"Very dull," the Viver replied. "Sometimes I can see the light of fires from the direction where we saw smoke earlier, but nothing else of importance. Some big flying predators flew by, but not close enough to be bothersome." The big Viver was standing easily on the steep-pitched roof cradling his heavy forcebeam, his eyes darting restlessly here and there independent of one another.

Kelly began pacing the terrace, idly counting his circuits, until he realized that it was lulling him into a trancelike sleep. He turned his attention instead to his surroundings. In the distance, he could make out a faint fireglow at one of the other platforms. His eyes traveled beyond, then suddenly jerked back. He had seen something move. He looked carefully, then saw it again. Something reflected the fireglow and it was hovering about fifty meters above the platform. For a moment, lights flashed around the thing, then it settled from view.

"Torwald, K'Stin! Look over there!" The boy pointed to where he had seen the phenomenon.

"What do you see?" Torwald asked. Kelly described what he thought he had seen.

"Might have been one of those flying predators K'Stin was talking about." Torwald shrugged.

"What about the lights?" Kelly's anger was mounting.

"Reflections from the fires, or maybe they signal like a lightning bug."

"Or maybe the little one doesn't see so good." K'Stin snorted. "Sentry duty should be left to those with senses sharp enough for it."

"No, I think the kid saw something. Anyhow, as long

as the thing doesn't get close, there's no sense worrying about it until morning."

For the rest of his watch, Kelly kept turning his eyes toward that far spectral stone platform, but he saw no more of the hoverer. He knew that he had seen something, though, and that it hadn't been an animal. He was sure that it had been a mechanical device, and that didn't help his peace of mind at all.

They rose early, wanting to reach the other ruins before the worst heat of the day hit. They were not much refreshed by the night spent in the stifling, bug-ridden humidity. Something had bitten Sergei, swelling one side of his face painfully, and Michelle had injected him with anti-allergens. It was decided that, to save time, they should split into two teams.

"Tor," said Ham, "you're in charge of the B team. Take Finn, Kelly, Nancy, and B'Shant."

"We do not separate!" said K'Stin, "Never!" Both Vivers began fingering their weapons truculently and looking very deadly.

"Well, then, Tor," said Ham, "it looks like you just have to get along without a Viver. Why don't you take Homer instead?"

"Fine with me. Homer's a better conversationalist, anyway." He looked over his team for a moment, then signaled for them to follow him out onto the terrace. "Now we'll get a chance to see if you really spotted anything last night, Kelly." Torwald turned and recorded a bearing on the platform with a directional indicator.

They descended the pyramid and crossed the platform in the direction of their goal. A sizable section of the masonry had fallen away at that point, leaving a precipitous but negotiable route to the ground. Without enthusiasm, they headed into the jungle once more. There were more open trails than they had found the day before, but dense areas were frequent, and they had to resort to the machetes. Without the Vivers to wield the big jungle knives, the work was slow and exhausting. First, Tor and Finn chopped away, then Nancy and Kelly took their places. Torwald demonstrated how to use the tools with greatest efficiency, but it was excruciatingly hard toil. At first, all did half-hour stints with the knives. Then they worked for twenty-minute spells. Finally, none of them could work much more than ten minutes at a time.

Just after midmorning, Torwald called a halt in a small clearing. "We'll break here for an hour. We don't have far to go now, and there's no sense killing ourselves." They flopped to the ground of the small clearing, reaching for their water packets. They drank slowly, swallowing salt tablets, replacing the moisture and salt they had lost through excessive perspiration.

"A fine lot of intrepid explorers we look," Finn commented while eying his bedraggled companions. "Did Columbus have such a crew? Or Amundsen? Was stout Cortez followed by such a ragtag lot? If we ever get back, who'll believe that we've been to the places we've been to, or seen the sights we've seen? There's not a single clean-cut, government-issue explorer among us."

"They'll have to believe us," Torwald replied. "We're making a visual record. Besides, according to my reading, explorers tend to be a pretty scrubby lot as a rule; misfits who're always looking for a place to fit in."

"That's us, all right," Nancy said ruefully.

Homer, who had been resting with his multitude of legs folded beneath him, suddenly shot to his full height of about two-thirds of a meter. Several of his antennae were pointing toward their destination and quivering. "I hear sounds of activity, not animal but organized."

"Well, we were pretty sure there were intelligent inhabitants there," said Torwald. "We did see smoke and lights from their fires—and *somebody* has Lafayette."

"These sounds carry tones of discord," said Homer.

"A battle?" Kelly volunteered, "Maybe two villages are fighting it out."

"I think not. There is sorrow, and anguish, and something I cannot place."

"Well, let's go take a closer look," Tor suggested. "Everybody on your feet and move out, but slowly and very quietly."

They picked up their packs and their weapons. Back in the jungle, they now tried to edge around tangled spots instead of hacking through them. Soon, they came to cleared land, like paddy fields sprouting tall brown stalks. The exploring party skirted the fields, keeping to the trees. They were almost within sight of the platform city when they saw the first natives.

About twenty of them were working in a field, tall and angular, body surfaces dull-green articulated plates. From the neck down, they rather resembled Vivers, but their heads were antlike, with a double-domed cranium bearing a deep crease down the middle. The crease was surmounted by a stubby crest, and they had four eyes apiece.

"Well, now we know who built the cities," Finn said. "Technologically speaking, they seem to have come down in the world. Are those stone tools they're using?"

"We can't be sure of that," Nancy whispered. "The builders might have chosen to portray one of their deities or demons with these people's features. What do you think, Tor?"

"This subject fascinates me no end. Let's get moving along. We just want to scout out the area, look for signs of the kid, and head back. Let's just go and get a closeup view of the city."

They passed the fields unseen and soon were in sight of a village built against the side of one of the great stone platforms. Taking to a deep ditch, they crept forward until, screened by reeds, they had a closeup view. The settlement was composed of about a hundred reed huts on stilts, thatched with broad leaves. The villagers were more interesting. A large party of them were working under the eyes of watchful guards, and the guards did not appear to be of the same species as the workers.

The new aliens had large, high-domed heads with broad, almost square snouts set with needle-pointed teeth. Three eyes were set above and to either side of the snout. Their upper torsos had four arms, the upper pair stout and muscular, the lower pair thin and delicate. Their legs were short and bent at the knee joints, the thighs thick and gnarled with muscle. The feet resembled an eagle's but had a large central pad for walking purposes. They sported long tails that appeared to be prehensile. Most disturbing of all, the beings carried efficient-looking weapons, rifles of some sort cradled in the upper pair of arms, and numerous smaller hand weapons hung on the harnesses that crisscrossed their bare torsos. Several carried swords as well as knives and clubs.

"Homer," Torwald whispered, "do you recognize those beauties?"

"Quite clearly. Those are Tchork. They had an extensive empire of nearly a thousand worlds—their policy is one of pillage and enslavement. As soon as they have exhausted a planet's easily lifted resources, they usually leave for better pickings, at least until the population has produced another stealable supply. They are a savage race who made it into space by serving as soldiers for more-civilized peoples. Once they had mastered the skills of spacefaring, they simply mutinied, stole the ships they had been serving on, and went into business for themselves."

"Just the kind of folks we needed to run into while our ship's disabled," sighed Tor. "Now, what do you suppose they are doing in this backwater?"

"They seem to be looting that city," Finn suggested. "Reasonable enough, when you consider that we had thoughts of doing just that ourselves not so long ago."

From where they stood, Torwald's group could see

that a rickety system of zigzag ladders and platforms reached from the village to the top of the platform, and two files of natives, one ascending and one descending, were using it. Those going up carried empty baskets, and those coming down were bent under full ones. The natives dumped the contents onto a pile growing in the center of the village. One of the Tchork appeared to be keeping a tally of what was dropped. The heap seemed to consist mostly of glittering metals, but there were also gemstones and objects not identifiable at a distance.

One of the natives staggered under the weight of his basket and lurched into the tallykeeper, spilling his basket in the process. The Tchork gave vent to a series of shrill barks and slapped the native so powerfully that the arthropoid nearly fell to the ground. When the native began to chatter in protest, the Tchork drew a heavy, cleaver-shaped blade and sheared through the creature's thin neck with one swipe. Sheathing the blade, the Tchork kicked the head across the village clearing and returned to his task. The line resumed its endless toil.

"Sweet people," Torwald commented. Nancy and Kelly looked ill.

"I suggest that we leave this place, and speedily," said Finn.

"No argument, there," Torwald said. "Now, very, very quietly, I want you all to turn around and start heading back the way we came. Stay low, keep your eyes open, and keep moving. If you see or hear something, use hand signals instead of talking. Maintain five-meter intervals." That last instruction reinforced the seriousness of their situation. The five-meter interval was an ancient footsoldier's practice to prevent having one shot or explosion kill two or more men.

Retreating slowly, bent over at waist and knee, they began sweating from more than humidity. All except Homer had the twitchy feeling between the shoulder blades that comes from leaving an armed enemy at one's rear. Had they been properly trained, Torwald would have had them crawling on their bellies. Once they were within the first line of trees and well out of sight of the village, Torwald called a halt. Taking out his communicator, he sent a distress alert.

"I hate to do this," he said to the others, "but they have to be warned in case we don't make it back." While his party was mulling that over, the response came through.

"What's wrong?" It was the skipper's voice.

"Tor, you in trouble?" That was Ham.

"Skipper," Torwald began, "be ready to clear out of here at a second's notice, repairs or no repairs. We've run into bad guys."

"Natives?"

"No, the natives are primitives. They appear to be peaceful farmers. The baddies are from elsewhere. Homer calls them Tchork and he says that they control a powerful empire. He also says that they're savages who've seized somebody else's advanced technology. From what we've seen, they're meaner than four-headed rattlesnakes." He described the scene in the village.

"That explains the condition of the city I'm in," said Ham. "All the valuable metal has been stripped away from the buildings we've explored so far. No gems, either. Nothing much left except stone."

"Listen," Torwald said, "we're heading back for that first city. Skipper, what shape's the AC in?"

"Won't be ready for several hours yet. It might be flying by the time you and Ham rendezvous."

"Let's hope so," Torwald said. "I'm signing off and getting out of here."

They made the best time they could getting through the trees. Chancing upon a well-marked trail that led in the right direction, they set out at a slow lope, fear overcoming their fatigue. Suddenly, without warning, a party of natives appeared around a bend in the trail and stopped, staring at the intruders. The humans also stopped, unsure what to do next. Then they heard an unmistakable, high-pitched bark. The natives scattered as two Tchork strode forward from behind. They, too, goggled for a second at the unexpected visitors, then raised their weapons. Biting back a curse, Torwald sliced one nearly in two with his beamer, while Finn shot the other neatly among the eyes with his pistol.

"Damn! That tears it! Run like hell, and don't stop till I tell you to." They flew down the path in desperation, running until their lungs were bursting and their sides felt as if they had red-hot knives in them. They came to an abrupt halt when the trail opened onto a broad clearing.

"We'll have to go across," Finn suggested. "The jungle's so thick here it'd take us an hour to get around."

"We'll go across one at a time," said Torwald. "Finn, you go first and cover the rest of us from the other—"

"Listen!" said Homer, antennae quivering in the direction they had just come. There were unmistakable sounds of rapidly nearing pursuit.

"On second thought," said Torwald, "we'll all go across at once. Keep your heads down and move!" They shot out into the clearing, spreading out and sprinting for the trees on the far side. A rushing noise sounded behind them and they were quickly enveloped in shadow. Looking back over their shoulders, they saw a many-sided craft hovering ten meters above the ground behind them, blocking the sun. Torwald and Finn turned and dropped to one knee, firing at the craft. After a moment's hesitation, Kelly and Nancy did the same. Their beams seemed to have no effect and were absorbed without damage by the bottom of the craft. Something large and amorphous was flung over the edge of the hovering craft. It spun toward them, spreading and whirling, a vague, transparent mass that hissed as it fell. The explorers scattered, but not quickly enough. They were borne to the ground by the surprising weight of the thing, which proved to be a net of fine, transparent, amber-colored strands. As they tried to raise their weapons, the net tightened, binding their arms tightly against their sides. In seconds, they were completely helpless.

The vehicle lowered to the ground, and a half-dozen Tchork jumped off. More came from the woods. Very carefully, they began extricating the humans from the sticky folds of the net, touching it here and there with a short, rod-shaped instrument which caused the meshes to fall loose wherever they were touched. Gingerly, the Tchork gathered the humans' weapons before freeing them. Once the humans were free of the net but under heavy guard, the Tchork lifted a large box off the vehicle and opened it. The net flowed across the intervening distance and swarmed into the box.

"That thing's some kind of animal!" said Nancy.

"Just the thing for capturing slaves without damaging the merchandise," Torwald said bitterly. One of the Tchork barked viciously at them, and they shut up. Kelly looked around for Homer, saw him nearby, placidly munching grass and trying to radiate an impression of utter, mindless stupidity. A Tchork in a jewel-studded weapons harness walked over to the crustacean and kicked him in the side. Homer ambled over to where his friends were being guarded. "Well, it was worth a try," he said. The bejeweled Tchork began barking again. To the humans' surprise, Homer began translating simultaneously with the Tchork's barks, so that there was no lag in transmission.

"Do not take me for a fool," the Tchork said to Homer. "I have seen your kind before. What are you doing here and what are these creatures? Our slaves captured one yesterday, and they say they have never seen one before."

"I am a poet, like most of my kind, and I travel in search of material for my verse. These persons are on business of their own and have been kind enough to allow me to travel with them." This time, Homer was speaking in two languages at once, a virtuoso performance.

"And what might that business be?" The Tchork

glared at the humans, who found a three-eyed glare to be a distinctly uncomfortable experience.

"We are explorers," Torwald said, extemporizing for all he was worth. "One of our number strayed from our ship, and we have come looking for him. I understand that you have him. If you'll just turn him over to us, we'll be on our way."

"Do not try my patience," the Tchork snapped, slapping Torwald solidly. "You are heavily armed."

"These jungles are full of dangerous creatures. Of course we're armed," Finn explained, as Torwald seemed slightly dazed.

"What world are you from? I've never seen any beings quite like you before."

"Our world is called Earth," said Finn, seized with a sudden inspiration. "It is the head of an empire of thousands of powerful worlds. If harm comes to us, they will take a terrible revenge on you."

"I do not believe you," the Tchork stated. "Besides, it was you who killed two of our men." He seemed fractionally less arrogant, though.

"They reached for their weapons first. What were we supposed to do?" Finn was playing the scene by ear, trying to find words that would be effective to this creature's peculiar psychology. "Besides, they were just lowly slave-drivers, beneath the notice of any person of quality." He was sure that humility would cut no ice with the Tchork.

"They were of no great value," the Tchork admitted, "but I am shorthanded here." He stopped abruptly, thinking perhaps he'd said too much. He switched subjects. "How many of you are on this world, and where is your ship?"

"Have we asked you such questions?" Torwald asked, seemingly recovered.

"You will do well to notice which of us is armed. Just answer my questions."

"We were left here by our ship several days ago to

make our preliminary survey. It will not be back for thirty more days."

"Then you must have a camp. You are not carrying enough equipment to last for thirty days in this terrain. Anyone can see that you are not creatures adapted for the jungle. Where is your camp?"

"I cannot tell you that until I am assured of the benevolence of your intentions."

Homer squawked slightly. "Torwald, I fear that there is no word in the Tchork language for benevolence."

"Hm, that figures. Try 'lack of immediate hostile intention' then."

Homer complied.

"Then you are protecting others. Or else you fear for the safety of your ship. You will return with me to my base. Get aboard!" They had no choice but to comply. Aboard the craft, they were seized and their arms bound behind them. Two of the Tchork kept them under watchful guard at all times. The craft lifted silently and turned toward the plundering site.

"Well," Torwald remarked in a half-hearted attempt at joviality, "at least we know now what it was Kelly saw last night."

They were worn out, aching, and filthy. The boss Tchork had been interrogating them since they had arrived back at the village, and the inquisition had not been gentle. Obviously, the Tchork were experts at dealing with many types of physiology, because they managed to be brutal without causing any really permanent damage. After fruitless questioning, the officer ordered them bound and placed between the stilts of one of the huts. No doubt, he did not wish to do anything drastic until he received instructions from superiors.

"Well, it could be worse," Torwald observed philisophically. "If they knew more about our anatomy and psychology, they'd know to stick burning slivers under our fingernails, or crush our—"

"Don't talk like that!" Nancy shuddered. "It was bad enough as it was. I think I'm going to lose a few of my teeth." She wiggled her jaw experimentally, probing at the loose teeth with her tongue.

"Michelle will implant some new ones for you when we get back to the ship."

"What makes you think we'll get back?" Kelly asked testily.

"No, no, you have it all wrong, Kelly," Torwald said. "It's you young ones who're supposed to be eternally optimistic, while we crusty old spacers are full of sour pessimism. Admittedly, our situation just now is eighty-twenty in favor of pessimism, though."

Torwald looked out over the village, where the natives were going about their endless drudgery. For about the fifth time that afternoon it began to rain and the villagers donned long, woven-grass capes. Evening was coming on, and with it some slight abatement of the day's heat. A mild breeze began blowing. Soon the natives started fires.

"I wonder if they plan to cook us," said Nancy.

"Don't be so morbid," Tor cautioned. "We saw fires from here last night. Pretty soon, they'll be toasting the local equivalent of marshmallows."

No one bothered to feed the Earthpeople. They also ignored Homer, who was kept in a small metal cage at some distance from his friends, where his nippers could not get at their bonds. Most of the natives huddled dispiritedly around their fires, while a majority of the Tchork had disappeared into a large, domed structure built against the base of the stone platform. Apparently the building was their barracks. The six guards detailed to watch the prisoners sat in a small group about a fire, conversing in low barks and growls. Occasionally, one would get up to check the prisoners' bonds. For a while, the guards killed time by playing a complicated game involving tossing counters from one prehensile tail to another. The player who dropped a counter or missed a catch was soundly kicked and beaten by the others. Eventually, the troopers tired of this and began a rhythmic barking and howling that might have been singing.

Despite the discomfort of their position and the pain of their treatment, the humans began to drowse toward midnight. Their guards were still wide awake and perfectly alert, and the prisoners had given up planning escapes involving sleepy guards. As he was about to drift off, Torwald's attention was caught by two natives who were walking between the huts, wearing rain capes and carrying grain sacks on their shoulders. One of the guards saw them also, and seemed suspicious. He barked and got to his feet, gesturing for the two to approach the guards' fire. The natives hesitated, then complied. Yes, Tor thought, those two definitely look odd. When the two were standing amid the guards, they suddenly dropped the sacks and capes. Instead of a pair of passive, obedient natives, the Tchork were staring in bewilderment at two specimens of prime, aggressive young Viverhood.

As the standing Tchork opened his snout to bark, K'Stin gave him a backhanded swat that sent him pinwheeling across the clearing. B'Shant gave another a kick in the snout that straightened him up to tiptoes, then lashed him across the midsection with a sidewise slash of a leg-spur, neatly disembowelling the guard. With two short, vicious slashes of his open-clawed hands, K'Stin killed two more Tchork before they were quite on their feet. Simultaneously, B'Shant grabbed another by the neck, snapping whatever served it for a spine, while the Viver's other hand drew a machete and with one lightning move halved the remaining Tchork from shoulder to waist. All six guards were dead. The entire action had taken about two seconds. None of the guards had managed to make a sound.

Quickly, the Vivers ripped open the sacks and re-

140

moved the weapons inside. While hanging various lethal objects about their persons, the Vivers set about releasing the prisoners. "You squishy people must not be very alert, to be caught so easily," K'Stin said cutting Finn's bonds with one razor-taloned forefinger.

"You know," said Nancy, "for the first time, you two look beautiful."

"We've always been beautiful, spongy yellow creature. Enough of aesthetics. Where is your gear?"

"I saw them take it over there." Kelly pointed to a hut fifty meters away. "A few Tchork went in that one with our stuff and they didn't come out again. They must be keeping guard on the stuff. I think that's where they have Lafayette, too. I saw a Tchork up there earlier tossing out an empty ration packet. They probably wouldn't be eating our food."

"Then we will have to kill more." K'Stin made a rasping noise that might have been a laugh. "Good." He and B'Shant crossed the clearing to the other hut without making a sound, keeping to the shadows. Ignoring the ladder, they swarmed up the stilts and dashed into the entrance. A faint scuffling sound was heard briefly, then silence. Carrying large bundles, the Vivers emerged a few seconds later. Sliding back down the stilts, they returned to the others and dumped their loads on the ground. One of the bundles groaned faintly.

"The prodigal returns," Torwald announced. The former prisoners picked up their weapons and equipment. "Leave the body armor. We can always make more back in the ship. It'll just slow us down, here." They were readying to leave when a group of Tchork emerged from between some huts, about a dozen led by some kind of petty officer. The intruders froze for a second, taking in the new situation.

"They're changing the guard!" Torwald cried. "Shoot!" He leveled his beam rifle and fired, as did the others. Before they all dropped, the Tchork managed to get off a few wild shots, sending jagged green beams sizzling through the air. None did any harm, but the racket brought their comrades boiling from the barracks.

"Run for it!" Torwald shouted, as the Vivers lofted a few grenades at the barracks. Flashes from the explosions lit their way as they stumbled toward the jungle. In a few minutes, they were joined by the Vivers, who loped easily into the lead, with Lafayette slung over B'Shant's shoulder. "Follow us!" called K'Stin.

In a small clearing, screened by some hasty camouflaging work, they came upon the most beautiful sight of their lives—the *Angel*'s atmosphere craft. They all swarmed aboard, Homer making a leap that seemed impossible for a creature with such short legs.

"Let's get out of here!" yelled Torwald. "They're right behind us!" Torwald could see Achmed at the controls and Ham manning a heavy cutter-burner mounted on a tripod in the tail section. Both men were in full armor, including helmets.

"Everyone back here!" bawled Ham. "On your bellies and aim to the rear!" Fighting their fatigue, the rest did as they were ordered; those not already equipped with rifles grabbed them from a stack in the cargo well. As the AC rose, a group of Tchork emerged from the trees. Ham cut loose with the cutter-burner, its searingly bright purple beam lashing among them like a scythe through grain. Marksmen were firing from the trees, and the human contingent fired back whenever they could spot a target. The Vivers methodically picked off snipers as soon as their sensitive eyes detected a flash. Ham cursed as a thin beam burned a chunk from the armor over his shoulder and swung the cutter-burner toward the shot's source in the trees. Fifteen or twenty trees went down in a heap, smoking and sputtering.

From his position prone by the controls of a jury-rigged rocket launcher, Torwald's eye caught the gleam of jewels, reflecting the light of forcebeams and brush-fire. He grinned suddenly. "Next time, show a little less vanity, sucker." He aimed directly for the biggest jewel. The beam must have started a chemical reaction within the stone, because the woods were suddenly lit bright as day for a millisecond as an explosion ripped through a circular area of jungle and clearing for a radius of six meters from the spot where the officer had been standing.

"Tor, what the hell was that?"

"A lucky shot, Ham—that's all." By then they were flying above the trees and almost out of range of the few parting shots thrown by the Tchork. Some of the less experienced humans began to relax, but Ham got them back behind their sights immediately.

"Back on your bellies and keep your eyes open! Nobody takes a break until we're back in the *Angel,* off this planet, and preferably in hyper away from this system. We're not out of this yet." As if to prove his point, an ugly, silent shape appeared a half-kilometer astern—the Tchork flying craft.

"See what I mean? Let her get a little closer, if she can. It's too dark to find good targets. You Vivers got any flares?"

"Naturally. We have some that are infrared. If they cannot see in that range, it will light them up for B'Shant and me, while leaving them blind."

"It's a good idea, but they may be able to see infrared as well as you do. In any case, us ordinary-type humans will need visible light to pick targets."

"The hull of their craft is immune to lasers and forcebeams," Torwald noted. "We found that out when they captured us. Maybe that cutter-burner can do the job."

"We'll give it a try," Ham said grimly. "That flitter looks open-topped. Is it?"

"There's a shallow well for passengers and cargo," Finn said. "It doesn't seem to be a military craft. There's a fairly high windshield forward, I don't know if it's beamproof like the hull."

"We'll soon know," said Ham. "They're getting close. You people with rifles watch for targets. K'Stin, B'Shant, loft me a couple of flares over that thing."

The tiny rockets arched above the AC. Set by the Vivers, they ignited just as the pursuing craft came under them, lighting it up most satisfactorily. The flares then fired small directional rockets, keeping them poised above the pursuers. Some of the Tchork tried to shoot the flares down, but the tiny targets were impossible to hit because wind buffeting caused them to dance from side to side.

"Fire!" Ham shouted, cutting loose with his massive weapon. The beams from the rifles seemed to have no more effect against the transparent windshield than they had had against the hull. The cutter-burner was likewise futile. After a few searing blasts, Ham stopped trying. "Torwald, you got a fine touch with frag rockets?"

"Better than most."

"Then loft me one just over that craft."

Torwald took a careful sighting at the ever nearing Tchork craft, examined the panel before him, set the controls for proximity and altitude, and punched a button. A moment later, a terrific explosion went off, several meters behind the pursuing craft. Torwald reset his instruments. He hit the button again. This time, the rocket ignited directly over the Tchork, at less than three meters. The concussion and spray of deadly fragments sent broken bodies flying over the bulwarks to crash into the jungle below. A few seconds later, the craft nosedived down into the jungle, sending up a spout of flame and a shattering roar when it hit. The crew aboard the AC cheered madly.

"Shut up and look to your weapons!" Ham shouted. "Good shooting, Tor."

"Took you two," K'Stin commented. "Waste of a good rocket."

"We all have our bad days," Torwald acknowledged. Within a few minutes, the welcome sight of the

Space Angel appeared before them. The AC flew into the lock at nearly top speed, decelerating so quickly that most of the people stationed aft came tumbling forward with their stored-up momentum. It was a masterful piece of flying on Achmed's part, and not until the hatch was shut and secured was he willing to collapse and admit that he'd been hit.

"Get away from him," Ham ordered quietly. "All of you, get to your stations, Michelle, bring your emergency kit, he caught it through a lung." At that moment the skipper dropped into the dock, her cigar at a 45-degree angle.

"Think he'll live, Ham?"

"Old Achmed'll make it, Gertie." Ham cradled the tiny Egyptian while bloody froth bubbled from Achmed's lips. Michelle reappeared with some esoteric equipment and shooed the rest away. The bridge officers prepared the ship for takeoff as Michelle and Torwald strapped Achmed into a bunk, with tubes sprouting from his slight body and transparent, jellylike plasters slapped upon his chest. When all was secure, the ship lifted off, wobbling and rattling from its uncompleted repairs.

"Everybody to battle stations," came the skipper's voice. "Forget about acceleration gear. We may be shooting our way off this planet, so keep your posts until we're safely in hyper."

"Kelly, come with me." Torwald then climbed the ladder toward the astrogation bubble where the controls for the new heavy weaponry had been installed. Torwald strapped himself into the chair behind the depolarizer console. As Kelly took the chair beside him, Torwald began checking out the controls. "Let's go through a test sequence, kid." Kelly began setting up imaginary targets, lighting up the viewscreens with blips and odd shapes traveling at different speeds and in wildly differing directions, some taking evasive action. One by one, Torwald obliterated the nonexistent attackers using the manual controls, then he set up the same problems and let the computer do the shooting. All systems checked out.

"Alien vessels coming over the horizon," the skipper reported. Tor and Kelly were quickly joined by Ham, who took control of the cutter.

"I don't have much faith in this thing," the mate said, "not after the way that craft absorbed the lighter cutters. I imagine their ships are made of the same stuff."

"That was my thought," said Torwald. "If they're made of ordinary molecules, though, this depolarizer should disintegrate them."

"That thing doesn't have much range, unfortunately," said Ham.

"There they are!" Kelly pointed out two large blips on the targeting screens. They tracked across the grid, slowly closing the distance between themselves and the freighter.

"Not fast, as warships go," Ham commented calmly, "but faster than the *Angel*."

"They've fired something at us," Kelly announced. A high-resolution screen showed four small blips fast approaching the *Angel*.

"Pretty slow," Torwald observed. "Must be torpedoes. See if the cutter can damage them." Ham set his sights and fired. Beams from four of the hex mount's projectors lanced out and destroyed the torpedoes.

"Whatever that armor is, it must be too expensive to waste on torpedoes." Ham's voice was beginning to reflect his excitement.

"More torpedoes coming!" Kelly said, "Much smaller, and there must be a hundred of them!" Ham and Torwald immediately turned their controls over to the computer, which could target and fire both weapons hundreds of times faster than any human. Within seconds, the small torpedoes were merely diffuse patches on the screen, whereupon both alien vessels put on a burst of speed.

"We're in trouble now," Ham said without inflection.

"They're going to try to close and use beam weapons. Two to one, and they're shielded against our cutters. Tor, try a torpedo."

"Torpedo away." One of the Class K subnuclear devices sped toward the pursuers. The torpedo's velocity, added to that of the alien ships speeding toward it, closed the distance rapidly and it was very near the vessels before they managed to destroy it. The detonation appeared to damage one of the ships. Its motion became erratic and it began to drop back.

"That's odd, Tor. They must not've licked the Doppler problem yet."

"Stolen technology, Ham, remember? These clowns can handle the ships, but they're probably not up to the mathematics necessary for computer ballistics." Suddenly there was no time for conversation, as the nearer alien vessels opened fire with beamers. The Tchorks' aim was not very precise, but, eventually, they were sure to score a hit. As predicted, Ham's cutter was useless, and the *Angel* was sure to be destroyed long before the alien got close enough to use the depolarizer.

"Another torpedo, Ham?"

"Might as well."

"Belay that!" The skipper's voice rang from the intercom. "We're turning and heading for them, collision course."

"Is this some sort of suicide tactic?" asked Torwald.

"Shut up and listen to the skipper," Ham growled.

"As Ham pointed out, Tor, those turkeys have trouble hitting something that's headed straight for them. If we reverse direction, we just might get close enough to hit them with the depolarizer. Anybody got any better suggestions?" There were none. Without bothering to decelerate, the skipper put the *Angel* through an end-for-end turn, maneuvering so that the *Angel* was masked for a time by one of the planet's small moons. It was the kind of maneuver made possible only by the invention of the gravity field. Without it, the crew would have been reduced to jelly and the ship turned to scrap in a millisecond.

When next the aliens had the *Angel* on their instruments, she was headed straight for them for a few seconds; they fired wildly, then the aliens were within range of Torwald's depolarizer. He pressed the firing stud, and the nearer alien very suddenly seemed to become much larger. The blip on the screen expanded and became too diffuse to show any shape, and then there was nothing. The farther ship shifted course and headed away, presumably going back to its home base. A concerted cheer over the intercom momentarily overloaded the speaker in the bubble.

"All right, all right, calm down," the skipper said. "I'm not handing out any cigars until we're safely in hyper. Stand by your stations."

Bone-weary, they sat around the mess table, downing cup after cup of strong black coffee. Numbly, they had downed the rations that Michelle had laid out for them. She refused to budge until they had all eaten and taken the medication she had prescribed. Now they were waiting for Michelle to return with a report on Achmed and Lafayette.

"That was a splendid piece of piloting, Skipper," said Sergei. "Tell me, just what kind of craft did you serve in during the War?"

"Oh, I piloted a Marauder. Ham was my master gunner."

"That explains a great deal."

Indeed, it did. The small, heavily armed craft had spearheaded nearly every fleet action and planetary invasion of the conflict. They were considered absolutely necessary—and totally expendable. And they had been expended at a terrible rate. Fewer than 10 percent of the personnel who served on Marauders had survived the War.

Everyone looked up as Michelle entered. "Achmed'll pull through," she said, drawing coffee from the bulkhead spout. "Lafayette's just bruised and battered. He'll be okay." There was a general sigh of relief from around the table.

"That wraps it up, then," the skipper said, lighting up a fresh cigar. "Any other reports or questions?" She looked around the table for a response, but with the exception of Michelle, Sims, and the Vivers, all of the crew members were slumped in their chairs or face-down on the table, sound asleep.

Seven

Repainting the hold had been a disagreeable job. With months on their hands while the *Angel* continued her random search for a solution to the problem of the Guardian, Ham had hit upon the bright idea of having Kelly and Lafayette scrape the old paint off the hold and repaint the whole thing. It was not, officially, an act of punishment. However, both knew that, had they not caused quite so much trouble on the jungle world, they would have been spared this particular task.

Kelly had washed up and put on clean clothes and was enjoying having nothing to do. Since they had recovered Lafayette, no one had referred to his blunder, although the hold-painting project demonstrated that his misbehavior had not been forgotten. Suddenly he heard a scuttling noise behind him, and Homer appeared at the hatch of his cabin. Teddy sat perched on Homer's shell. "What sadness lengthens Kelly's hours?"

"Homer, have you been going over that Shakespeare stuff again?"

"It has a certain precision and beauty of expression that is lacking in your present language."

"Well, no sadness is lengthening my hours. Relief from scraping paint is shortening them, if anything."

"Then why are you brooding?"

"Like everybody else, I guess. We could spend the rest of our lives out here without finding a good decoy to distract this Guardian. What could occupy something that powerful for any length of time?"

"I see." Homer extruded a tiny-fingered hand on a long arm with six elbows. He used it to scratch Teddy's ears. "I often forget how important these time spans are to you humans. Let me see . . . the Guardian will attack a single ship that strays too close. It will engage a fleet, also. Suppose a truly enormous fleet were to approach, spread out on a wide front. Might that not occupy the being long enough for Sphere to accomplish his mysterious purposes?"

"Maybe. I don't think anybody would lend us a fleet, though, Homer. Especially since it would be destroyed."

"We might find such a fleet, though."

"Huh? What are you getting at?"

"I have heard many rumors and poems concerning planets converted into gigantic fleet bases at some far distant date in the past. Often, the ships found there are still operational and have been utilized by races such as the Tchork that can build no better craft of their own."

"Can you find one of these planets, Homer?"

"One of the poems gives a set of coordinates . . . they will have to be translated, of course; they would mean nothing to your computers." Homer began to mutter to himself, but by that time Kelly was out the hatch and headed for the bridge.

Nobody could believe the screens: monstrous floating docks, surrounded by quiescent fleets of ships, stacked level on level, dwindling beyond the range of human eyesight. A monitor would hold on a particular formation for a few minutes, then switch to another. Each screen registered at least ten such installations per minute.

"The planet's the same way, folks. Nothing but spaceports from pole to pole."

The crew remained silent for a few moments, then Ham spoke up. "I don't think all the ships I saw during the whole War would amount to a single one of those floating fleets. I think we've hit the jackpot."

"You suppose we could get some of those ships moving?" Torwald's expression and tone of voice betrayed his doubts.

"You'd better hope so," the skipper replied. "Enough to distract the Guardian, anyway. We could get awfully old looking for a better prospect. I intend to locate the biggest of the ground installations —that'll be the likeliest place to find a headquarters. After that, we'll just have to play it as we find it."

"We've found the place," the skipper announced. "Biggest spaceship installation imaginable. There's a mountain sticking up out of it and we'll land on top of that. It's the only spot for a hundred kilometers around that isn't sealed under metal. The people who built this must have stripped this whole system of metals. It's unbelievable." The skipper turned to Torwald. "Put together a ground party. Make it a small group, this time, three or so besides you. The rest can help put the final repairs on the ship."

"Right. Finn, were you planning anything for today?"

"To be sure, my jewel, I was planning to work on my memoirs, but I can spare an hour or two."

"I appreciate it. Kelly, you can come along. And you, Nancy. We'll take the Vivers, just in case. Homer, how about you?"

"I would be most willing to go. I would be little help in repairing the ship, I fear. Also, I should like to see this world. A planet of such sublime devotion to a cause must be most inspiring."

"We don't need inspiration," the skipper said. "We need a nice quiet place to repair the ship and figure out a way to distract the Guardian. This looks like it."

Torwald pointed to Nancy, Kelly and Finn. "All right, then, you three get your gear together. Nancy, round up K'Stin and B'Shant. Kelly, put together some emergency rations from the galley and load them in the AC."

Kelly went to the supply room and checked his equipment. He and Torwald had fabricated new body armor to replace what had been abandoned on the jungle world. He helped Nancy with hers, and they inspected the gear they would be taking. The heavy packs they had taken before wouldn't be necessary since they would be traveling by AC. All the heavier equipment they might need—axes, spades, crowbars, and the like—went into bundles to be stored in the AC's cargo space.

The intercom tooted twice and Ham's voice rang through the ship: "Planetfall in thirty minutes. All hands to quarters and strap in."

Kelly trudged aft to his cabin and strapped himself into his bunk—an awkward procedure in his bulky armor. He lay back and stared at the overhead. He wondered whether this would be their last planetfall before returning to Earth. Earth seemed curiously remote, now. The ship was his home, not the planet where he had been born. He remembered the day in the spaceport, when his adventure had begun. Probably close to two years, now. He thought to check it out on the bridge, then discarded the idea. It didn't really matter, anyway. Suddenly the landing klaxon blared and his mind was on other things.

Torwald and the skipper were standing in the AC bay hatch when Kelly and Nancy arrived. Kelly threw his bundle into the AC and pushed his way forward to see what the two were staring at. His eyes widened like theirs.

"What's it look like?" Nancy asked as she shoved past Kelly. "Oh," she said in a small voice as she reached the hatch.

It was a sight to take the breath away. The landing site was the flat top of a mountain overlooking a flat plain five thousand meters below. They could sweep at least a hundred kilometers with their eyes and every square meter was covered with ships or spaceport facilities. Not only the plain but also the mountain were covered with docks, hangars, landing pads, and structures of indeterminate function.

Towers like splinters of steel thrust into the cloudless, yellow sky, some of them far taller than the mountain peak upon which the *Angel* rested. Ships of all sizes and shapes marched row on row to the horizon. Everywhere was the gleam of metal. Except for the small patch of bedrock beneath the *Angel,* not a scrap of nonmetallic material could be seen. The structures began just a few meters downslope from the *Angel*'s resting place.

"Okay, Tor, you and your team pile into the AC and start looking."

"What exactly are we looking for, Skipper?"

"How should I know? Look for something that doesn't look like everything else. There must be some kind of command center on this planet, and this is the biggest installation around, so it's the most likely spot to check out first, Now, stop jawing and get to work. Call in when you find something interesting."

"This could get tiresome." Torwald climbed into the AC. The others piled in with him. They needed no breathing equipment on this world, so they were mercifully spared the necessity of wearing enclosed helmets, although they were taking along battle helmets in case of trouble.

"What keeps the oxygen level so high?" asked

Kelly. "Nancy says the vegetation's too thin to account for it."

Torwald was interested. "That so, Nancy?"

"Right. No oceans, therefore no plankton to account for it. No forests or grasslands. Most of the planetary surface that isn't sealed under these spaceports is rock desert."

"How about bacteria?" asked Finn.

"Maybe, but it would have to metabolize at a tremendous rate to make this much oxygen. By rights, the oxygen content of this atmosphere should run a fraction of 1 percent. Instead, it's nearly Earth-normal."

Kelly turned to the crablike alien. "What do you say, Homer? Ever run into anything like this before?"

"Quite possibly. However, it's not a subject I delve into very much. Poetry is my main interest, so I rather seldom bother with things like atmospheric composition."

Finn chuckled. "Great. We have among us what may be the galaxy's most widely traveled resident, and all he's interested in is poetry."

"When one visits as many worlds as I do, it is best to specialize."

Torwald nodded. "He's got a point there."

Installations flowed endlessly beneath them—ships, hangars, fueling-stations, and what appeared to be repair shops—but there was no sign of life.

After several minutes Finn turned to Nancy with a puzzled look on his face. "Strange. It'd look just like a Navy installation at one of the big wartime bases, but there's nothing that looks like barracks, or offices, or messhalls. Not even a latrine."

Nancy nodded. "Maybe the creatures that built this facility didn't need such things."

"Maybe they were robots," Kelly added.

Torwald listened to the speculation with some annoyance. "Maybe this is all hallucination! Let's go down and have a closer look. We'll try that ship." He directed the AC toward one of the taller ships: a flat-sided spire with featureless metal hull plates. It stood on thin, stiltlike legs that seemed too fragile to support its bulk. Next to the ship sat a low, domed structure.

Torwald squeezed the AC alongside the small building and all got out to have a look around. They could find no access to the building, so they turned their attention to the ship itself. The vessel was, likewise, devoid of hatches.

"Why did they hide the entrances, Tor?" wondered Nancy.

"Didn't want intruders, I imagine. Come on, let's try someplace else."

They spent much of the day checking out more of the buildings and ships. The result was always the same—buildings and vessels were sealed. Torwald finally ordered a return to the ship. On the following day they would return with the shortbeams.

Torwald stood on a jury-rigged platform at the base of one of the tall ships, hefting a cutter. "I hate to do this, Skipper. Seems a shame to take a cutter to a perfectly good ship."

"Just do it," her voice said tinnily from their radio receiver. "It wasn't going anywhere, anyway."

Torwald made a preliminary cut. Nothing untoward happened, so he expanded the slice into a continuous rectangle. When the metal cooled, he attached clamps and lifted the section free. Inside, a maze of pipes and cables was visible, but little else.

"I don't see any deck." Kelly craned his neck and directed a light upward. "No ladders or any other kind of footing, either. What kind of creature used such a ship?"

"Creatures without feet, probably," Nancy offered.

Torwald turned to Homer. "How about taking a

look inside? You can get around in there, and we can't."

"Certainly." The alien extruded several climbing limbs and scrambled inside. Kelly managed to keep him centered in the beam of the searchlight until Homer disappeared into the upper reaches of the ship. He returned a few minutes later.

"What did you find?" Torwald asked.

"Very little. There seems no provision for life at all. What seems a guidance center is located in the center of the ship. It is a metal box about the size of your head. No life-support mechanism, no writing that I could detect in any visual range. I think this must be a robot ship."

"I wonder if they all are," said Kelly.

"Let's try a building," said Torwald.

They tried several. Once again, they had to cut their way in. None of the buildings had visible entrances, exits or windows. Inside, they found instruments, power plants, fuel, reactors, repair shops for the ships, but no sign that life had ever been there. There were hangars with maintenance facilities for many types of ship, all of them fully automated.

"I don't get it, Torwald. The ships we found in space were abandoned because of an emergency. But this place? It's like somebody built it and forgot about it."

"I know, Kelly I—" Torwald cut off short as a distant roar sounded. They ran to the AC where the others were gathered. K'Stin and B'Shant sprang to the weapons.

"It comes from above!" said K'Stin. "North and 95 degrees." They all searched the northern sky. "I can see it on infrared," K'Stin exclaimed "a bright light, swiftly descending."

By then the others could see it, a bright point of light, roaring louder as it neared the ground.

"Get this thing off the ground and head north at low speed," ordered Torwald.

"Is that a ship landing, Tor?" The skipper's voice came through the AC speaker.

"Looks like it, Skipper. I'd be willing to bet it's from one of the formations in orbit."

"Most likely. I hope we haven't attracted notice."

"Not likely. With all the firepower around here, there'd be no reason to bring a ship out of orbit. I'll bet it's just routine maintenance. If so, that ship's getting orders from somewhere. See if you can get a bearing on a transmission. It could save us years of searching this planet."

"Good idea. I'll get right on it."

"Meanwhile, we'll go check out this ship. Torwald out." He turned to his search party. "How far, Finn?"

"About twenty kilometers due north. We'll be there in a few minutes."

They sped toward the spot where they had lost sight of the descending light only to find a huge depression filled with housed machinery of incomprehensible function. When they arrived, the ship had already set down, one of the small, round variety. But that was not what attracted their attention. The ship sat on a metallic apron, and around it bustled machines, most of them rolling on soft tires, attaching cables and hoses to fixtures in the hull of the vessel. The majority of the items being attached rose from the apron itself. The machines operated smoothly, efficiently, in almost complete silence.

"It's spooky, Finn," Kelly said. "They don't make any sound."

"They must be self-servicing, repairing and maintaining each other long after their designers have forgotten them, or died off."

"It is unseemly that mere machines should possess such longevity." K'Stin's bearing reflected disgust and frustration—emotions normally foreign to Vivers. After a few minutes, the wheeled machines pulled away from the ship and the apron slowly began to sink. The ship gradually disappeared into a well, and when its nose had cleared the rim, a cover slid out and closed over it.

"Drydock!" Torwald yelped. Suddenly a beep sounded from the AC transceiver.

"I've got a fix on the control center," the skipper announced. "It's on the other side of the planet. Return to the ship."

Back aboard ship, the skipper briefed them on the latest findings. "This planet is covered with ancient mining operations." She hit a switch, and the main bridge screen displayed a panorama of an abandoned open-pit mine. "This is a detail of one of the pictures we took from orbit. There's nothing to judge scale by here, but that pit's six kilometers across. No sign of mining equipment, and it's ancient. See the erosion around the rim. Sergei says on this planet that means the pit was excavated at least twenty tousand years ago. And the planet's covered with 'em. What do you make of that, Homer?"

"I think I may have an explanation. An ancient poem comes to mind."

"Let's hear it," said Ham. "Always liked poetry, myself."

"I fear that some of the nuances would escape you. It is in a sixteen-tone language, and the proper effects are achieved by speaking words in pairs, each unit of each pair being enunciated in eight of the tones, the other in the other eight."

Bert coughed, fought to suppress a laugh. "A subtle form, true. Perhaps a translation then?"

"A recitation would take some years."

"Give us a summation of the pertinent verses," Michelle urged. "The suspense is killing me."

"Long ago, there lived a great and powerful race, masters of many star systems. They engaged in a war with another species—over what disagreement the poet knows not. The first race was far less numerous than the other and sought to compensate by raising great fleets of warships that required no living beings to be operated. They refined this practice to such a degree that, not only were the fleets self-operating, they were also self-constructing."

"Self-constructing?" The skipper arched an eyebrow.

"Yes. Even so. In the van would go the construction vessels. They would land on a suitable world and locate mineral deposits, their machines would gather raw materials. They would then build factories, which would produce warships, their necessary support apparatus, and more construction vessels. When all was completed and in readiness, the construction vessels and ancillary machinery would move on, leaving behind a world turned into a gigantic military base, awaiting orders to attack. The poet says that these facilities continued to be constructed long after the war was over, even after the races themselves had vanished into oblivion. It is said that the Center is dotted with such bellicose relics, but in all my long lifetime, this is the first evidence I have seen to indicate that the poem was based on true events."

"Thousands of years," the skipper said, "and it's still operational."

The control center was disappointingly small. To control a whole planetful of spaceports and all the fleets in orbit, the crew had expected something the size of the major Earth spaceport. Instead they found a low dome about thirty paces around. Torwald, the tallest of the standard humans, could see over it easily.

Place me on the dome.

K'Stin was the only one whose reach was long enough, and he gently set Sphere on the center of the dome. Instead of rolling off, Sphere stuck to the dome as if glued. Time passed.

I am ready. Return me to the ship.

They started involuntarily. Sphere's communications had been so infrequent in recent months that they had grown unaccustomed to the sudden intrusions of its mental thrusts.

"Maybe this is it, Tor."

"I hope so, Skipper. I'm beginning to miss the fleshpots of civilization."

K'Stin returned with Sphere and positioned it on the mess table. Around the mess, the crew waited attentively. The being held in its power their return to human-controlled space. Without its help, they would be lost, drifting helplessly among the stars like the derelicts they had encountered. If it had at last found a means of accomplishing its mission, they felt they might be able to return with some of the wealth they had found. There was a good deal of tension in the air as they awaited its decision.

I think I may have found a decoy sufficient to distract the Guardian.

There was a general releasing of long-held breath.

The vessels of this facility are fully functional.

"All of them?" the skipper was aghast.

That is correct. In addition to those on and in orbit around this world, others are on or orbit the worlds, and satellites of this system. All have been well maintained since their construction.

"How many?" asked Torwald.

Seven million, eight hundred thousand, four hundred twenty-two. This figure includes warships, cargo carriers, and tenders.

"Can you get them all launched?" the Skipper asked.

I have begun the launch sequence. The command instrumentation has been cleared of its former data and reprogramed with my instructions. When the

161

fleets are in space, I shall convert their engines to the power system that now moves this ship.

"And then?"

Then we go to the Core Star.

Kelly, Torwald, Nancy, and Michelle sat in the navigator's bubble, downing coffee. Homer sat on one of the gun controls, sipping a mixture of prussic acid and turpentine which seemed to be making him a bit tipsy. With Homer, though, it was hard to tell.

"This is most exhilarating. Like an old epic. In all my wide experience, no race has ever attempted a feat as heroic as diving into the Core Star with nearly eight million ships, to do battle with the Guardian."

The others favored him with looks of little enthusiasm. Finally, Michelle spoke. "In our experience, nobody's dived into *any* star and survived."

"One hopes that Sphere will be able to cope with this difficulty," said Homer.

"One hopes, indeed." Torwald snorted. "I, for one, have my doubts about that talking football's ability to preserve us from frying."

Homer's visible antennae quivered. "It does seem to have some extraordinary capabilities, though." The crustacean extruded a siphon and sipped delicately at the turpentine.

"Nearly eight million!" Kelly's voice was a hoarse whisper. "That'll be a sight." He turned to Michelle. "How many ships do you think the human worlds could get into space at one time?"

"I once saw nearly four thousand in mass formation. That was before the Li Po invasion. Of course, not many of those returned."

"And this is just one installation," said Nancy. "Do you think humans will ever achieve such power, Tor?"

"Probably. We made it through the last couple of centuries without wiping ourselves out, hard as we tried. There's nothing to stop us from doing this

kind of thing, given time and inclination. I do hope
we put our efforts to less pointless uses, though."

"So great a quantity of ships is rather unnecessary,"
said Homer. "Especially as none of them have anything to do."

"Well, they have a job now," Torwald said.

The stars, which had seemed fixed above their
heads, began to shift. Nancy was the first to notice.
"The skipper's rotating the ship."

The edge of the nameless planet rose into their
view, ascending until its full bulk hung over them, a
great, baleful globe encircled by the brilliant stellar
display of the Center. The rest of the crew began
drifting into the bubble. Last of all came the skipper.
"We're about to witness a fantastic display. Keep
your eyes on the planet."

They watched. Nothing happened for a few minutes, then a tiny, brilliant white dot shone against the
featureless yellow. Immediately dozens of other dots
appeared, then hundreds, then thousands, and still
they increased, until the whole hemisphere was alight,
covering the face of the planet in a web of diamonds
as spectacular as the stellar backdrop.

"Three million ships from this planet. A million and
a half from this hemisphere alone. All lifting off at
once." The skipper was awed and said nothing more.

"Such a massive departure will alter the orbit of
this planet forever," Bert mused. As the dots length-
ened into fiery trails, the planet became almost painful to look at.

"Where do they all rendezvous?" Finn asked.

"They'll mass in a parking orbit near the biggest
orbiting station, the one in the most distant orbit from
the planet—look, the off-planet fleets are moving
now."

Flashes from locations in space near the planet were
adding to the dazzling visual effects.

"We'll pick up the rest from the other planets as

we leave the system. Those are already heading for rendezvous along our path."

"Then what?" Kelly asked.

"Then Sphere jumps the whole mess into his brand of hyper and we all go pay the Guardian a visit."

The bridge was quiet. Kelly was standing watch with the skipper, his eyes restlessly moving from one screen to another. He was fascinated by the sight of the massed fleets. *Space Angel* had rendezvoused with the last divisions and was waiting for Sphere to finish programing the ships. From the bubble, only a few of the nearer vessels could be discerned, but the telescopic screens could scan hundreds of thousands at once.

Torwald entered, carrying several coffee cups. Kelly felt that he would be happy if he never saw so much as a single coffee bean as long as he lived. The other crew members, Navy veterans all, seemed to require the stuff to live. Torwald handed a cup to the skipper, who sat with her feet propped on a console while she brooded over the sight of the incredible fleet.

"*Your cup,* Grand Admiral Gertie HaLevy! How does it feel?"

"It feels like I'm a passenger, Tor, just like the rest of you." She growled the words around her cigar, her chin sunk nearly into her jacket.

"Must be discouraging."

"Biggest fleet in the galaxy out there, and I'm not even in control of this little tramp freighter." She snorted disgustedly. "Grand Admiral my—" Her words cut off as the images on the screen flickered, distorted, seemed to lengthen, then disappeared. The screens and instruments went into the familiar convulsions brought on by Sphere's hyperdrive.

"Last leg of the trip in, folks," Torwald announced.

The skipper made a sour face. "I wonder if there's going to be a trip back."

Kelly felt his mouth become dry as he contemplated an unpleasant conclusion to his first space voyage. "What are our chances, Tor?"

"I'd say just about zero. But, then, I thought that a lot of times during the War, and here I am." The skipper nodded agreement. Kelly had to be satisfied with that.

Eight

Kelly was killing time by going over navigation tables when Sphere's "voice" rang through the ship.

If you wish to view the Core Star for yourselves, you may do so. It is within sight now.

Kelly swallowed hard. He was not so sure he wanted to see this. It might be like staring back at a firing squad. "Oh, might as well," he said to himself. He slowly rose from his bunk and stepped to the hatch, first checking to see whether his face was too pale. He didn't want to disgrace himself. In the companionway he met Lafayette and Achmed. Achmed was still bandaged, but mending fast. At least, Kelly thought, the engineer had an excuse to look a bit shaky.

They found the others on their way to the Navigation bubble. For once, nobody seemed anxious to see what new wonder the dome was to reveal.

They filed through the hatch and into the observation chamber. The ship was canted so that they didn't have to crane their necks to see the phenomenon. "Phenomenon" was the only word Kelly could think of for this sight. He had been expecting something blindingly bright, like Earth's sun, only infinitely larger. It was not like that at all.

What he saw was a flattened ball, taking up much of space in the quadrant visible from the bubble. The ball was not bright, but it was somewhat painful to look at. At first, Kelly thought it looked a dim blue, then he decided on purple, no, gray. He finally decided the thing had no color at all.

"It's like looking at an ultraviolet lamp," he said. "It's more like I can *feel* it than see it."

"What's radiating from that thing isn't properly light at all," Sergei said. "A thing of that mass should suck up light like a black hole. You'll notice that it seems dim, yet we can see no other light source, even though this is the center of the galaxy."

In his wonderment at the Core Star, Kelly hadn't noticed, but it was true; all of space around the Core Star was perfectly black. Not a star was visible. Within the Core Star, however, an endless play of the nonlight was taking place. It flowed and coalesced in a most disturbing manner, changing intensity from moment to moment. Kelly felt slightly ill watching it.

"What's keeping us alive?" asked Torwald.

I am.

"We were wondering when you'd speak up," the skipper said. "Are you satisfied now? We've taken you where you wanted to go. This seems to be the center of the galaxy. Can you get us back to human-occupied space, now?"

There yet remains a task.

"I thought there'd be a catch."

"We've got a visitor," Michelle said, staring at the hatch. The others followed the direction of her gaze. Sphere floated through the hatch about two meters from the deck. It halted in the center of the chamber.

"I was under the impression that you couldn't get around by yourself."

So near the Core Star, I already begin to strengthen.

"What's this last task?" Anger made the skipper's voice tremble.

This ship must accelerate directly into the Core Star.

"Enough!" K'Stin shouted suddenly. "We consent to risk! We do not consent to suicide! You soft ones may accept death at the command of this absurd spheroid, but Vivers do not! He would murder not only us, but all our progeny."

Simultaneously the Vivers reached for Sphere, then froze in midreach, as if turned to stone.

Have no fear. They are immobilized to prevent them from doing something foolish. In their dim way, they understand what is transpiring around them.

"I wish I could do that," the skipper said regretfully.

"Now, Sphere," said Torwald, "this business about diving into the Core Star. Couldn't you just go by yourself, and pick us up after you've finished your business there?" The others nodded hopefully at this suggestion.

I fear not. If my protection were removed, you and your ship would instantly be reduced to your component atoms, and the atoms themselves destroyed and transmuted into Core Star matter.

"Just a suggestion."

"Sphere," said Homer, "can you tell us why? What events led us to this singular fate? Before we take this ultimate step, please tell us what you are, and what the Guardian is, and the nature of the Core Star."

Very well. But words are a clumsy conceptual tool to convey such information. At best, your minds can perceive only the dimmest glimmer of this tale. When it has been revealed to you, you will be nearly as ignorant as before.

"Tell us anyway. We deserve at least that much."
Very well.

They were the collective consciousness of the crew of the Space Angel, *and they were in the center of all matter. This they could not see, but could perceive through knowledge and senses not their own. Here was the one Mass of matter in the universe, formless, without dimension, for there was nothing else in the void with which to compare, only the Mass, and nothing. They knew, as one knows in a dream, that this Mass would create the universe they knew.*

Then, the Mass was not One any more, but an infinity of fragments hurtling in all directions from the center. The fragments split and subdivided, collided and shattered. Gradually, the expansion began to slow. The formlessness of the original Mass, the chaos of the explosion, yielded to a new factor—Order.

Pieces of matter began to coalesce, larger attracted smaller. Much of the original material was a fine dust that fell toward strong centers of gravity. Dust and chunks of undifferentiated matter became roughly spheroid masses. Smaller bodies orbited larger. The systems thus formed arranged themselves in groups of millions and hundreds of millions, billions and trillions around yet a greater center of gravity. These supergroupings evolved into lenses and vast spirals. Still, all was shrouded within a cloud of fine particulate matter.

Then the crowning transmutation occurred. The masses of matter impacted upon one another with incredible pressure, as the matter tried with mindless intensity to reach the center of gravity. Molecules were crushed out of existence, the atoms themselves compressed so that even these basic units could no longer stand the strain. Collisions began to occur.

As the reactions took place, one by one, the greater masses burst into a glory of flame. Now they were stars. The first gust of solar wind blasted the clouds of dust from the new star systems. There was light in the universe, no longer formless matter, but stars and galaxies, still expanding, still under the impetus of the great explosion that had created the universe.

In the very centers of the new galaxies, phenomena were developing that did not obey the rules of the rest of space, rules that had begun with the explosion of the original Mass. These were the Core Stars.

In the original explosion, not all of the basic matter had been blown to dust and gas. Some accretions of primal mass remained relatively intact, and these had generated the gravitational cores around which the galaxies had formed. The cores existed within real space, yet apart from it, their rules and processes as alien as those of the original Mass. They were too great, too massive, even to exist in real space. Restraints such as mass, energy, time, did not apply to these superstars. In their chaotic wells, amid speeding particles, another, unique factor began to occur: intelligence.

Within the core of a giant galaxy, a great mind flashed into existence, the inevitable result of an ordered arrangement of waves and particles, an ultimate coherence among the random patterns of the rest of existence. The immense Core Star became self-aware. Shortly afterward, it became aware of another like itself.

The great intelligences of the Core Stars became known to one another. The basic rules of existence in the universe were apparent to them, so they wasted little discourse on these matters. All of what later and lesser species arising from the primal explosion would call knowledge and culture was self-evident to the beings of the Core Stars. Even so, among them were those who wanted more, beings analogous to the psychopathic members of later, less evolved societies.

The Guardian was such a being. Once like the other Core Stars, a shining standard of brilliance among the luminous minds at the centers of the great galaxies, it began to crave power. Power was a thing of no account among the Core Stars, for all were of godlike potency. This state was not enough for the one who became the Guardian; he wanted dominion over his fellow intelligences.

Seeking this power, he committed crimes incomprehensible to creatures of human intelligence, crimes many and heinous. It became necessary for the others to take action. A battle was fought, one on a scale so great and under conditions so alien to human thought that only the fact of conflict was even comprehensible to humans.

The warped Guardian fled.

A Core Star mind was appointed pursuer, the being that would one day be called Sphere. Eons earlier the stellar minds had learned to detach themselves from their Core Stars and travel freely among the galaxies and in other-dimensional realms. Mass, energy, time, were things over which the stellar beings wielded almost complete control.

Sphere searched. But it had one weakness common to all the Core Star minds: Away from his Core Star, he weakened. Slowly but inevitably his powers diminished. One way existed to renew those powers. Though only the greatest galaxies had developed intelligent Core Stars, the smaller ones had lumps of primal matter at their cores. They lacked the titanic stresses that had called into being the great minds, but possessed sufficient energy to resuscitate a wandering Mind.

When Sphere felt himself weakening past the point of safety, it was necessary only to bathe in the Core Star of a smaller galaxy. However, on one occasion, Sphere miscalculated and headed into a Core Star, only to find that the Guardian already occupied it. They fought. In its weakened condition, Sphere could not prevail. While it still had sufficient strength, he had to break off and flee. The Guardian became the pursuer.

The battle lasted eons by human standards, the flight, further eons. Finally, rather than risk destruction in meeting its enemy too soon, Sphere hid in an insignificant planet with the requisite materials.

Sphere compressed himself into the smallest practicable size, then embedded himself in a slab of the hardest substance he could create from the materials at hand. After many billions of years, gravity would inevitably draw the planet and its star back into the core. But the unexpected occurred: Tiny beings with just the glimmerings of intelligence found him. His wait might be over.

"Unbelievable!" Bert exclaimed. "A thinking star! A creature that can wrap a planet around itself like a blanket and sleep for a hundred billion years." He shook his head in amazement.

They were all a little dazed by the tale. It was as if eons had passed, yet as if no time had passed at all. While lost in their shared vision, they had been perceiving the passing of ages from Sphere's time scale, wherein time had scarcely any meaning at all.

"Well," said Torwald, "we begin to understand."

You are scarcely able to understand at all. You have had a tiny glimpse of our existence. Possibly, you understand as much as humans are capable of.

"What next?" the skipper asked.

The fleet has been transported to the side of the Core Star opposite us. It is my hope that it will occupy the Guardian long enough for me to join with the Core Star, so that when he finds me, I shall have regained enough strength to do battle.

The skipper was not pleased. Her face grew red and the forefinger of her right hand tapped impatiently at the staff of the bubble. "And if he's not delayed long enough, if he doesn't fall for the decoy?"

Then I am doomed.

"And so, incidentally, are we?"

Naturally.

"When does it start?"

We are accelerating toward the Core Star now. The fleet has already begun its attack.

"When will we know?"

It hardly matters. If the Guardian prevails, it shall be as if you had never existed.

"Nothing like a pep talk from the commander," Torwald muttered.

Then they were heading in. The Core Star loomed visibly larger through the bubble while the assembly watched. There was no sensation of movement, no vibration within the ship, no sound.

The silence was broken abruptly by a sudden exclamation from Nancy. "What's happened to Sphere?"

The others turned from the dome and stared at the spot where they had last seen Sphere, but found instead a nebulous cloud of multicolored flame, rapidly expanding. The phenomenon grew to fill the room, seemed to pass through the viewers without effect or sensation. When the room cleared of the dazzle, they could still see it outside, surrounding the ship and growing ever larger.

Torwald was the first to recover his voice. "We're inside him now."

Outside, the fire blazed with ever-greater intensity. On the telepathic level that Sphere had used to communicate with them, they began to experience empathetic stirrings, a vicarious sharing of Sphere's sensations.

There was a tremendous, elated exaltation as the godlike being renewed himself. New strength, new power, surged through his alien fabric. Soon, he would be able to meet his adversary on even terms. Time ceased to have meaning for the "spectators," as it had when they had experienced the history of the stellar minds. Without warning, Sphere's exulting ceased.

"The Guardian is here," Homer announced.

The conflict began. The strange beings attacked one another on many levels simultaneously—mental struggles, energy clashes on a multitude of levels of reality, some of which the humans were able to perceive only dimly. Psychic skirmishes occurred on planes for which human minds had no concepts, much less words.

Suddenly the crew members were out of the Core Star, situated on a plane that seemed like their own, amid the close-packed stars of the Center. Occasionally a star would flare nova brilliantly as the two beings drew on them for support in their struggle. The humans realized that this should not be possible; even with the stars so close, they should not be able to see so many explode at once, but in their new reality, time and the speed of light were not as before. Nebulae were sundered like spiderwebs by the violence of the battle. On this level, the beings were not themselves visible, but they were wreaking destruction at the Core that would be visible on Earth in a hundred thousand years. A momentary shift of plane revealed a "place" where the combatants could be seen as two monstrous masses of color that collided and shifted without mingling.

The warring became chaotic, incomprehensible. In the collective experiencing of the *Angel*'s crew, a new development was taking place. Images dredged from their unconscious minds began to appear. In order to make the battle even marginally comprehensible, their minds began supplying images from the mythic past of Earth.

On a tremendous plain, as featureless as a floor of glass, an armored figure on horseback warred with a jewel-scaled dragon, whose breath was a noisome, poisonous fog. The dragon's neck arched, its fearsome maw agape to snap at the knight, but a giant lance passed between its jaws and . . .

Another plain, but one covered with ice and surrounded by tall mountains. In the distance, a great wooden hall could be made out, and a bridgelike rainbow arched away to infinity. On the ice, a huge gray-bearded man, one-eyed and wearing a golden helmet, did battle with a slavering wolf. The wolf's nostrils spurted flame and its eyes were red coals. Where saliva from his gleaming fangs dripped to the ice, clouds of foul steam erupted. Man and wolf fought on interminably, the man's armor unbreakable, the wolf's hide impenetrable. But the man was tiring. Without warning, he slipped, fell backwards, and the wolf was upon him, fangs flashing as . . .

In an upland jungle a hideous demon stood, his lower body like that of a water buffalo, his upper that of a man. His face was that of an ape, with the tusks and ears of an elephant, and the horns of a goat. In his hands he bore a sword and shield. Against him rode a beautiful young woman mounted on a lion. She wore a crown, and from her torso sprang ten arms: two bore sword and shield; two drew the bow; one wielded the sharpened steel ring; one held an elephant goad; one a bell, one a bowl; one a mace; the last a prayer wheel. They battle continually until the demon crouched for one last spring and . . .

A giant stairway, kilometers wide, stretched below and above to infinity. In middle of the golden stairway two figures can be seen. The lower is a loathsome creature, its form unstable, difficult to distinguish but repulsive nevertheless. The figure above looks human, a body clad in raiment and armor so bright they are hard to look upon. But from the creature's shoulders spread immense and graceful wings, their feathers glinting with metallic iridescence. The face is human, but inhumanly beautiful, neither male nor female, as majestic as truth and as cold as justice. With both hands, it swings a titanic sword with blade of blinding fire. The dark being quails and shrinks, inching down the stairway. The evil one tries to rise but is repeatedly forced back, growing weaker and less menacing by the moment, retreating faster, then fleeing, and then . . .

Kelly came to with a jolt. He was on the floor of the navigator's bubble, leaning against the depolarizer consoles. He looked around. The others stared back at him, and at each other. The Vivers were in control of their bodies, but appeared uncharacteristically subdued. Only Homer seemed unchanged, and it was always difficult to tell about Homer anyway.

"It's over," said the skipper. "Sphere won."

"I witness that Allah is great," said Achmed, still in a daze. "I witness that He is One."

"Now what?" asked Torwald. Kelly had never heard the veteran spacer sounding so weary.

"That was the question you were getting so tired of," said Michelle.

Now I shall continue my task.

"But, you won."

Only this little skirmish. This business shall continue for some time before resolution.

"You didn't kill it?"

A stellar mind cannot be killed. We are immortal.

"Then, your objective isn't to destroy it?"

Not at all.

"What then?"

I must gain control for a time, then I must cure him.

The crew of the *Space Angel* sat in silence for a while, unable to absorb any new wonders.

"Then, you're a psychiatrist?"

That would be the closest human equivalent. I am a healer. The being called the Guardian is faulty, as are all his kind. The problem is still not completely understood. But we believe that a permanent cure is feasible. One day I shall capture him, and he shall become a stable being once again.

"And what of us?" The skipper's mind was always on business.

You are my last task. As I informed you earlier, I am only a tiny function of Sphere's mind delegated to deal with you. The Sphere being is still unaware of your existence. But he is nothing if not just. You have aided him in his task. Therefore, I shall set things right with you before I abandon this disagreeable form and experience and rejoin the great mind of Sphere.

When first encountered, you were collecting the crystal that enshrouded me. You shall return home with your crystal. You have spent some little time at this task, but I think that the artifacts and information you have garnered on this journey to the center of your galaxy shall repay your trouble handsomely.

Most important, you take with you this knowledge. In the center of your galaxy lies a Core Star, a phenomenon composed of the primal matter of the universe. The control of that matter makes all things possible. It shall be eons before your species can learn to utilize the Core Star, but when you do, all possibilities will be open to you. You can even hope to become beings such as myself. I now return you to your place and time, for time means nothing at the Core. Farewell.

They blinked and stared about. One by one, they wordlessly staggered to their feet. Nobody wanted to be first to speak. Suddenly their eyes were drawn to the planet hovering overhead, its blue oceans and white clouds nearly filling the view from the bubble.

"I don't believe it! That's Earth!"

"Ham, get to the bridge!" The skipper snapped out of her daze and became all business once again. "Get on the communicator and ask for instructions."

Ham had disappeared long before the skipper finished her orders. She seemed not to notice. She walked to one of the new terminals and slaved it into the bridge command consoles. A voice came through.

"What ship? This is Earthport Authority. I say again, what ship? You have dropped from hyper into orbit in an unauthorized and unorthodox fashion." The controller was obviously flustered. "Identify yourself immediately or be fired upon."

"This is the freighter *Space Angel*, Captain Gertrude HaLevy commanding."

There was a brief interlude as the unseen controller consulted his computer.

"Not the *Space Angel* that filed a spacing plan for Alpha Tau Pi Rho/4 under contract to Minsk Mineral?"

"Of course it's that one!" the skipper barked. "How many ships of that name have a skipper named HaLevy?"

"Have you been forced to turn back for an emergency?"

"Turn back?"

"Unless my readout is incorrect, you have not been away nearly long enough to have reached Alpha Tau and returned." The voice's intonation left no doubt as to what its owner considered the likelihood of a mistake by the computer.

The Skipper held her hand firmly over the mike, "But, we've been gone more than two years, subjective."

"*Space Angel!*" said the voice, "prepare to be boarded by security forces of Earthport authority."

The party from Earthport Security arrived in a swift, pugnacious-looking little cutter. The crew of the *Angel* assembled at the lock to greet them. First through the hatch was a gray-haired man in Port Authority uniform, followed by several armed men in police uniforms. Their businesslike advance stopped short when they caught sight of the Vivers. The policemen fumbled at their holsters.

"Easy, men. Those two are part of my crew." The skipper fought hard to suppress a smile.

"A . . . Captain HaLevy?" The gray-haired man obviously was quite nervous. "I'm Major Whipple, Port Authority, and I hold you responsible for the behavior of those . . . those creatures."

"Do not worry, shell-less one," said K'Stin. We shall not harm your men. The sight of them reaching for weapons fills us with mirth. We are amused."

"Hmm, yes, I suppose so. Now, Captain HaLevy, I noticed as we approached that your ship mounts some highly illegal weaponry."

"Oh, yeah, I forgot about that."

"I dare say. Now—" Suddenly, he caught sight of Homer. "What's this? An alien animal? I fear that it must be held in orbital quarantine, effective immediately. You know the regulations very well. My God! What an ugly creature!"

"Hey, you can't talk that way about old Homer." Kelly was quite angry. He patted the grotesque shell affectionately. "And you can't put him in quarantine like an animal, either."

"And why not, if I may ask?"

"Because, sir, I am a poet, and accustomed to receiving the honors due that profession. I take exception to your remarks."

The inspector jumped several meters, almost into the arms of the policemen. "It talks!" he yawped. "Is it intelligent?"

"That's debatable," Torwald exclaimed. "Depends on how you feel about poets."

"What's the meaning of all this?" Whipple was almost tearing his hair out by the roots.

Ham decided a cooler head was necessary. Palms outstretched placatingly, he approached the distraught Whipple. "Now, now, calm down. You see, it's like this . . ."

The last of the visitors were about to depart. For

two weeks, the *Space Angel* had been in a maximum-security dock in Earthport, her memory banks being examined by teams of State scientists. The crew had been subjected to endless interrogations until the authorities were satisfied that they had no more information to impart about their singular adventures.

Then the reporters and professors had arrived in endless numbers. Information about the *Space Angel*'s voyage was spreading through human-occupied space, her crew had become instant celebrities.

Kelly had been delegated the job of giving a small group a tour of the ship, showing off such of their souvenirs as had not been impounded by the government. Among the group were a man in uniform with the comets of an admiral and an official from the huge Satsuma Line. The ship's boy felt a bit overwhelmed; not long before, he had been just another anonymous orphan scrounging a living in Earthport, his highest ambition *any* job on any ship. Now he had important men hanging on his every word, his face would be known wherever humans lived.

As he conducted them from the ship, several took him aside for a few private words.

"Son, have you ever considered a career in the Navy?" The admiral was doing his best to be paternal.

"Sure. But I never could get past the recruiters."

"Something could be arranged. A few months in a special school, and you could be a commissioned officer."

"I'm really not interested in a military career any more, sir." Kelly was slightly embarrassed.

"Decided to stay on in the merchant service, eh?" The Satsuma Line man thought he sensed an opening. "Good choice. We'd be glad to have you in the line. Good pay, regular promotion, regular hours. And, I don't mind telling you, your reputation would move you on up ahead of some other men with a bit more seniority."

Kelly eyed the man's stiff, starched uniform, laden

with insignia of rank and accomplishment, and reflected that the line officer probably spent most of his time behind a desk.

"I hear Satsuma's a fine line to work for." Kelly was noncommittal.

"Keep us in mind."

Last to disembark was a short, bearded man in frayed spacer's gear. A ratty cap with a tarnished medallion pinned to the front sat jauntily atop his disheveled mass of hair.

"I don't know if you caught my name at the introductions," the bearded man said. "Captain Probert of the *Black Comet*. I've just bought the ship at an auction, and I'm putting together a crew."

He spoke casually and his relaxed manner immediately put Kelly at ease. "Independent freighter?" asked Kelly.

"What other kind is there?" Probert grinned. "You 'prenticed for the quartermaster this trip out, didn't you?"

"That's right, but, I cross-trained in most of the other ship's duties."

"I can always use a good hand. Pay's not like the Satsuma, we work for shares. Hours are long, but I've already got a good cook. Keep me in mind."

"Thanks. I'll do that."

When Probert had gone, Kelly trudged back to his cabin and stripped off his rented dress uniform. He climbed back into his familiar coverall and boots and looked at himself in the mirror. The outfit, which had sagged when he first put it on, now fit perfectly. The boots, which had once felt so heavy, now felt like old slippers. He grinned self-deprecatingly at his reflection and went to join the others. He found most of them around the mess table.

After a few moments, the skipper arrived. She seemed a trifle put out, and signaled for general attention. "Now that we're all here, we can come down off our cloud. We may be interplanetary celebrities, and we've brought back the most valuable treasures this planet's ever seen—not to mention our cargo of diamond crystal—but we're broke."

"Broke?" Kelly asked, "how's that possible?"

"The government can't quite decide what to do with all this unprecedented stuff, so they've just impounded everything, including the crystal, and they're going to sit on it until they think of something. In addition, the assets of Minsk Mineral have been impounded. We can institute lawsuits, and we will probably get everything we are owed, but be prepared for a long wait. Court actions such as this can last years. That means we've got to find another contract if we're to stay in business."

This was his moment. Kelly cleared his throat and spoke. "I'm afraid I won't be with you."

"What do you mean?" It was plain from the skipper's expression that she knew what he was going to say.

"Well, I want you all to know that this ship has been a home to me, and you've been like a family and I never had either before. But you can't stay at home forever. I signed on as ship's boy. You can't hold that position forever. I've outgrown it on this voyage."

The skipper looked to her quartermaster. "Torwald?"

"He has nothing more to learn from me. He could ship as quartermaster in any independent freighter and he pilots an AC like a champ."

"Look, Kelly," Nancy said, "you could sign on for another voyage as my assistant. There's a lot you don't know yet about Commo." To Kelly's astonishment, her look and voice were almost pleading.

"Thanks, Nancy," "but, I've got a chance to strike out on my own, and it's important to me to take it. I can't be carried on somebody's kindness forever."

"You have a ship in mind?" The skipper's voice was brusque. "Not a line vessel, I hope."

"Captain Probert's offered me a berth in the *Black Comet.* I think I may take it."

"Probert's a good man." The skipper held out her hand. "Give me your bracelet. I'll bring it up to date." She took the bracelet and left the room. As she walked down the companionway, the others could hear her honking into a handkerchief.

Sergei looked up from a sheet of printout he'd been examining. He smiled at Kelly, then said, "Minsk will set up a bank account for the *Space Angel,* into which we'll pay her share of the crystal's value, whenever it's released. If you like, I'll have a separate account set up for you."

"It'll be a pretty hefty sum," said Torwald, "when and if it arrives. It could be enough for you to buy into a partnership on the *Black Comet* or some other ship. Not bad for an ex-ship's boy just off his first voyage."

"That'd suit me," said Kelly. The skipper returned a few minutes later and handed back his bracelet. As he clipped it on, Kelly noticed the tiny silver star embossed on it.

"But, this is a Spacer First Class bracelet," he protested. "I should only be eligible for Able Spacer."

"As you pointed out, you only signed on as ship's boy for a routine voyage. It lasted a little longer, and you got some experience that most don't get. Going to the center of the galaxy and diving into a star might be considered above and beyond the call of duty. You've earned the promotion."

Kelly stuffed the last of his belongings into his spacebag. He had accumulated quite a bit—souvenirs from the worlds and alien vessels the *Angel* had visited, and gifts from his fellows. Lafayette, somewhat shamefaced, had visited Kelly's cabin and handed him a cube of glassite within which was imbedded a tiny sphere—it was the jungle planet, as seen from space. "I used Achmed's holography gear and the ship's computer to make it," Lafayette explained. "Under microscopic projection, the detail is perfect down to the plants and the ruins." Awkwardly, the redhead stuck out his hand. "Thanks for saving my neck. Sorry you ended up having to paint the hold."

The skipper had presented him with a box of cigars and Achmed a prayer rug—"in case you should come around to the true faith." Bert had given him a full set of cargo master's manuals, and K'Stin an efficient-looking sword.

Kelly made the ritual last-minute check around the cabin, the first room he had ever had to himself, ran his hand over the bunk and the shelves, then shrugged. Home was a spacebag now. He had his gear and his trade. What more did a spacer need?

The crew assembled at the hatch to see him off. There were handshakes and hugs all around. Tears in her eyes, Nancy threw her arms around Kelly, kissed him violently, and said she would miss him.

"I wish you'd mentioned something like that before."

"You weren't leaving before," she replied logically.

Homer scuttled up to him. From somewhere within his shell, he produced a recording disk. "This is a crude form of my epic, *Core Star,* in which you figure prominently. You may not be able to understand it, but rest assured that your immortality is guaranteed."

Torwald handed him a package. "Just a little something I whipped together in the shop." Kelly unwrapped it. It was a perfect model of the *Space Angel,* accurate down to the empty rocket-mounts. Kelly's fingers closed around it and he turned swiftly so the others couldn't see his face as he stuffed it into his spacebag.

"Maintain eternal vigilance, small squishy thing—"